CLAUDIA KISHI, MIDDLE SCHOOL DROPOUT

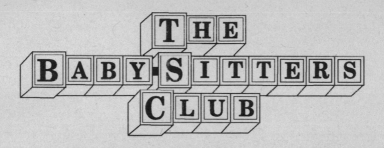

CLAUDIA KISHI, MIDDLE SCHOOL DROPOUT

Ann M. Martin

AN
APPLE
PAPERBACK

SCHOLASTIC INC.
New York Toronto London Auckland Sydney

Cover art by Hodges Soileau

ISBN 0-590-69207-0

12 11 10 9 8 7 6 5 4 3 2 1   6 7 8 9/9 0 1/0

Printed in the U.S.A.   40

First Scholastic printing, October 1996

The author gratefully acknowledges
Ellen Miles
for her help in
preparing this manuscript.

CHAPTER 1

"Using your protractor," I read aloud, "measure each angle." I picked up the protractor and glared at it. It had such a friendly rainbow shape, but it wasn't friendly at all. It was a hated enemy. Why? Because I didn't have the slightest idea of how to use it.

My teacher had gone over it, more than once. And there were even some directions in the math textbook on the desk in front of me. But I couldn't remember my teacher's directions, and the author of my textbook clearly doesn't speak English — at least, not the same English I speak. She speaks very good math, but that's definitely a foreign language to me.

I'm Claudia Kishi, and I'm thirteen and in the eighth grade at Stoneybrook Middle School, which is in Stoneybrook, Connecticut. You'd think that being in the eighth grade would mean I am capable of doing eighth-grade math, but so far that doesn't seem to be the case. It's October, and school's only been in session for a little over a month now. What I want to know is, how did I already become so hopelessly behind?

It's not just math, either. I feel lost in all my subjects. I'm being buried by earth science. I'm history in social studies, in which we're studying everything between the Civil War and now. And English? It might as well be Greek.

But you know what? This situation is really nothing new, nothing I can't handle. I've never been a star student, to put it mildly. My spelling is atrocious, I have the worst case of math anxiety in SMS history, and my attention span is about as long as a five-year-old's — unless the subject happens to interest me.

Here, in case you're wondering, are the subjects that interest me: arts and crafts of all kinds, kids, junk food, mysteries. Interesting list, isn't it? Notice how vocabulary building doesn't show up on it? Or protractor usage?

School just isn't my thing. Art is, and so is baby-sitting. (I belong to this outrageously great club called the BSC, or Baby-sitters Club, but more about that later.) And I'm basically addicted to any kind of junk food — whether from the salty, greasy, sugary, or chewy food groups — and to Nancy Drew books. My parents don't approve of Twinkies or mysteries, so I keep my supplies of both pretty well hidden.

In fact, I was just reaching for a Yodel (I'd hidden a package of them behind the thesaurus my parents gave me for Christmas last year) when the phone rang. My phone, that is. I have my own private line, which is way cool.

"Hello?" I answered it.

"So, what are you wearing?"

It was my best friend, Stacey McGill, and her question didn't strike me as odd at all. What we're wearing happens to be one of our favorite topics of conversation.

Not that we're shallow. We're interested in lots of stuff besides our appearance. But we both love clothes and jewelry and accessories. For me, they're just another outlet for my creativity. I see my body as sort of a blank canvas, a moving work of art.

Stacey, on the other hand, is coming from another place. Manhattan, to be exact. She's into clothes because — well, because she was brought up on an island where all the natives dress to kill, every day. I mean, have you ever walked down Madison Avenue at lunch hour? The sidewalk looks like a feature in *Vogue* magazine. It's filled with women who look like models, all wearing the very latest *couture*. That's where Stacey — who could be mistaken for a model herself, with her long curly blonde hair and blue eyes — is coming from. Her style is a lot more sophisticated than mine; mine is much funkier and artier than hers. We're perfect shopping buddies because we rarely dive for the same item. She'll be going gaga for some navy blue, Chanel-style blazer while I'm raving over a faded denim jacket with sixties-style embroidery on it.

Anyway, I wasn't fazed by her question. Though I have to admit, I was a little bewildered. After all, we'd seen each other at school only an hour or so ago. "I'm wearing the same thing I was wearing all day," I said, looking into the mirror as I spoke. "You know, my tie-dye leggings, black overall shorts, red high-tops — "

"I didn't mean what are you wearing *now*," Stacey interrupted me. "I knew that. And by the way, you looked totally cool today. What I meant was, what are you wearing to the dance?"

"Dance?" I asked.

"The Halloween Dance," she explained. "You know, the one they announced this morning."

"Oh, right!" How could I have forgotten? The announcement had been made during homeroom, while I was in the middle of trying desperately to finish homework for three dif-

4

ferent classes. I guess my mind had been else-where. "Good question," I said. "We'll have to come up with some awesome costumes. Do you have any ideas?"

"I was thinking about going as a flapper," said Stacey. "You know, one of those old-fashioned girls with the long beaded dresses?"

"Sounds cool," I said. "I haven't thought about it at all yet. I'm too busy trying to figure out how to use this stupid protractor." I picked it up and made a face at it.

"Oh, that's a snap!" said Stacey. "I can ex-plain it in about two seconds, if you'll listen closely."

"Uh, that's okay," I said. I've been *there* before. Stacey is a straight-A student in math; in fact, I think she's already taking some ad-vanced course like trigonometry. It comes nat-urally to her, and she thinks it's really easy. That's why her explanations never work for me. I don't think she has any idea how little I understand. For example, I'm still not exactly clear on what an angle is, or what it's for, or why I need to measure it in the first place. I could never explain that to Stacey. She'd be rushing on to tell me how to find the square root of the isosceles or something.

"I think I hear Janine, down in the kitchen," I said. "I can ask her."

"Okay," said Stacey. "Whatever. I guess I'll

see you at the meeting later, right? We can talk some more about our costumes then."

"Great," I replied. "See you!" I was glad she didn't seem hurt by my putting her off. It's just that school is always such a struggle for me, and if I started depending on my friends to help me, I have the feeling they might not be my friends for long. This was something I had to figure out on my own. I wasn't really going to ask Janine. Her explanations are even more complicated than Stacey's.

Janine's my older sister, and sometimes I feel as if I'm living in her shadow, at least at school. Every year my teachers start out thrilled to have me in their classes, because I'm Janine's sister and they all just adored her. (She's always been a straight-A student.) But within weeks, they've usually figured out that I'm not the scholar Janine is. It's not that I'm dumb, it's just that I don't care about facts and figures the way she does. I can't seem to work up a passion for fractions, you know?

On the other hand, my art teachers have always recognized that I'm talented, and that makes me feel great. I don't mean to sound conceited or anything. It's just that I seem to have this urge inside me, an urge to create. If you put a pencil in my hand, I draw. If you give me clay, I sculpt. Color and form and

6

texture are all languages I understand perfectly.

Anyway, back to Janine. She's a junior in high school, but she's already taking college-level classes. I bet she'll end up winning that Nobel Prize thing one day. Or she'll invent a new number, or discover a cure for the common cold. She's Smart, with a capital "S." In fact, she's an official genius. But I don't hold it against her. I like Janine. She's okay for an older sister.

The rest of my family consists of my mom, a librarian, and my dad, an investment banker. (My grandmother Mimi lived with us until she died not long ago. I miss her very much.) Also, my Aunt Peaches and Uncle Russ live nearby, and they just had a baby girl named Lynn. After me, I might add. Lynn is my middle name. I *adore* that child! I have Lynn's newborn picture taped up over my desk. She might look ugly and wrinkled to some people, but to me she's beautiful.

I gazed at her picture for a few minutes, forgetting about the stupid protractor. I was daydreaming about how much fun it will be to take her shopping (once she's old enough to walk, of course) and buy her cute outfits. I was visualizing her in a cowgirl look, with red boots and a red satin shirt, when there was a knock on my door.

"Come in," I said. It was Janine.

"Hi, Claudia, how was school today?" she asked.

I made a face.

"Need any help with your homework?"

For a second, I was tempted. Then I remembered how long-winded Janine can be when it comes to math. She loves the subject so much that once she starts in on it, you can't shut her up. Anyway, I was tired of the whole protractor thing and ready to move on, even if it meant I'd be even further behind in math class.

"No, thanks," I replied. "It's nice of you to offer, though."

"Sure," she said. "Anytime. I guess I'll go start dinner, then." She turned and left.

I closed my math book and cleared all my school stuff from my desk. Then I pulled out some drawing paper and my favorite Italian pastel crayons, and went to work on a project I've been thinking about.

I've been wanting to do a self-portrait. But this wouldn't be a picture of me, exactly. It wouldn't show my long black hair or my dark almond-shaped eyes (I'm Japanese-American, in case you haven't guessed by my last name). This self-portrait would show more about who I am than what I look like.

I wanted to figure out a way to capture feelings on paper, to show the world what I'm thinking. I wanted to create a self-portrait that would reflect me, Claudia Kishi, as I am right now.

In my art class this year, we've been learning about abstract art. Abstract art is "nonrepresentational" (big word, huh?), which means that it doesn't look like exactly what it is. In other words, if you paint an apple in the old-fashioned way, it looks just like an apple. But if you paint it in an abstract way, you use color and line and composition to *suggest* an apple.

I know, it sounds complicated. But to me, it's simple. And fascinating. (I guess that's how Stacey feels about math.) I couldn't wait to start my project.

I gazed at the blank paper, thinking about all that I wanted my self-portrait to convey. I wanted it to show my sense of style and my sense of fun, my deep family ties and my pride in my Japanese ancestry, my love for color and texture, and my connections with friends. That was a lot to pack into one little drawing, but somehow I felt I could do it.

CHAPTER 2

Once I started on my project, it was hard to stop. When I'm really involved in creating something, it's as if the world goes away and time stops. The house could practically burn down around me and I would barely notice. That's why it took my friend Kristy three tries to get my attention.

"Claudia!" she called. "*Claudia!* Hello, CLAUDIA!"

Finally, I looked up and grinned. "Hey, Kristy," I said. "Is it five-thirty already?" She was standing in my doorway with her hands on her hips.

"Five-twenty-five," she informed me. "You know I like to be early."

I started to clean off my desk. I wasn't ready to show anyone my project yet, and if Kristy Thomas was there it meant that all the other BSC members couldn't be far behind. It was time for a club meeting, and nobody likes to be late and face the wrath of Kristy.

The BSC was Kristy's invention, which is why she's president. Among her friends, Kristy is known as an "idea person." She's always coming up with these very simple yet totally terrific ideas. Since my friends and I love kids and baby-sitting, the BSC has to go down in history as the best Kristy idea ever.

Here's how it works: seven of us baby-sitters meet in my room (because of my private phone line, which earned me the title of vice-president) from five-thirty until six on Mondays, Wednesdays, and Fridays. Parents can call during those hours and set up sitting jobs. (We have two associate members, just in case we're overwhelmed with work. They don't attend meetings, but they're always standing by to help.) We keep track of our schedules in a record book, and we write up every job we go on in the club notebook. (Not exactly my favorite thing to do.) It's really very simple, and it works perfectly.

Well, almost perfectly. Recently there have been some glitches. In fact, for awhile there it looked as if the BSC's days were numbered. Everything was going wrong. We were fighting with each other, we weren't making time for meetings, and there were more than a couple of bad sitting experiences, including one in which a child was injured.

Things were so terrible, in fact, that Kristy decided the club was history. And none of us even put up a fight. We disbanded the club and went our separate ways, and we thought we were better off. It took a terrible accident to show us how much we needed and missed the BSC. We decided to start up the club again, but agreed that we'd take it slow and see how things went. So now we're on probation.

We haven't been meeting again for very long, and we still aren't totally comfortable with each other yet, but I think we're glad the BSC still exists. I know I am.

By the time I'd finished cleaning up, everyone had arrived. But you'd never know there were seven girls in my room. It just wasn't like the loud old days, when we'd all be giggling and talking at once as we waited for Kristy to call the meeting to order. There was no giggling, and nobody was talking much. When we did talk, it was with this slightly polite stiffness, as if we were talking to adults we didn't know too well. I pulled out my usual supply of junk food (Raisinets this time, plus some Smartfood cheese popcorn) and passed it around, and everyone was careful to thank me as they helped themselves. I think it's going to take some time for the BSC to be itself again. Still, I know we love each other, and we'll be friends forever.

12

I know most of the people in the BSC really, really well. In fact, I've known a couple of them — Kristy and her best friend Mary Anne Spier — since we were in diapers. So it wasn't a big stretch for me to imagine the abstract portrait I'd do of each of them. That's what I was doing as I looked around the room: trying to figure out what characteristics of each person I'd show using only color, line, and composition.

Kristy would be easy. In real life Kristy has brown hair and brown eyes, is short for her age, and dresses very casually in jeans and turtlenecks. Her portrait, on the other hand, would be a study in motion and chaos, suggesting a whirlwind of activity. Kristy's always busy with something, whether it's Kristy's Krushers, the little kids' softball team she coaches, or just her own family, which is huge. She has two older brothers, Charlie and Sam, and one younger one, David Michael, plus a stepsister and stepbrother who live with her every other month (Karen and Andrew), plus a toddler (Emily Michelle) Kristy's mom and stepdad Watson adopted. And then there's Nannie, Kristy's grandmother, who lives with the family, too. Not to mention the assorted pets! Fortunately, Kristy lives in a huge house. Actually, it's more like a mansion. Watson is really, really rich. But Kristy didn't grow up having everything she wanted. In fact, after her dad left (he took off years and years ago) Kristy's mom struggled to keep the family going. So they definitely deserve all the nice things they have now.

Kristy has always wanted the BSC to be the best possible club. She's constantly coming up with ideas to make us better sitters. Kid-Kits, for example. Those are boxes we've decorated and then filled with stickers, crayons, and hand-me-down toys and books. Kids are crazy about them. But even Kristy has had to realize that not every single one of her ideas is great for the club. The last one she had — the Fall into Fall Festival — was, well, a dud. Everyone's entitled to at least one bad idea, though!

Next, I studied Mary Anne, Kristy's best friend and the BSC secretary. (She's in charge of that record book I mentioned, and she does an excellent job of keeping track of our complicated schedules.) Mary Anne has brown eyes and hair, just like Kristy, but she has a trendier haircut and cares a little more about clothes than Kristy does. She and Kristy may look alike, but their personalities are like night and day. Mary Anne's portrait would have to capture her soft, tender personality. She's the most sensitive, caring person I've ever met. She's also shy, but once you know her you'll never find a better friend.

(I almost lost Mary Anne's friendship recently. She and I had a huge fight during the bad time the club went through, and I still feel terrible about it. We've made up, but I'm not sure if she's totally forgiven me.)

Mary Anne grew up as an only child with a single parent. Her mom died when Mary Anne was just a baby. Mr. Spier took parenting very seriously, so seriously that he almost didn't let Mary Anne grow up. Now he's not a single parent anymore, and Mary Anne's not an only child. Mr. Spier married a woman named Sharon Schafer, who happens to be the mother of Mary Anne's other best friend, Dawn (and of Dawn's younger brother, Jeff). See, Dawn and Jeff grew up in California, but their mom grew up here in Stoneybrook. When Dawn's mom and dad divorced, Sharon moved back to Connecticut, bringing her kids. She met up with her old high school sweetheart — Mary Anne's father — and ended up marrying him.

Mary Anne was thrilled to have a sister and brother. Unfortunately, though, it turned out that first Jeff and then Dawn discovered that they never really felt at home in the East, and both of them ended up moving back to California to live with their dad. Oh, they visit a lot, but their home is out there. I know Mary Anne misses Dawn a ton.

The phone rang as I was watching Mary Anne, and the BSC swung into action. Kristy answered the phone with a cheery "Baby-sitters Club!" and listened for awhile, then hung up after promising to call the client right back. "That was Mrs. Newton," she reported, "looking for a sitter for Jamie and Lucy on Friday night."

Mary Anne checked the record book, scanning it to see which of us was free. "Looks like the job is yours," she said, smiling at Stacey, who sat next to her on my bed.

"Great," said Stacey.

Kristy called Mrs. Newton back, and that was that.

Stacey is the club treasurer. She's responsible for collecting dues each week, which are used to pay club expenses such as my phone bill. It's the perfect job for Stacey, since math is so easy for her.

My abstract painting of Stacey would have to suggest her strength, beauty, and elegance. I've already told you what she looks like and how she dresses, but I haven't told you one important thing about my best friend: she has diabetes. That's a lifelong disease caused by her body's inability to process sugars correctly, and unless she takes really good care of herself every single day Stacey can become very sick.

Her parents, who were divorced not long

16

ago (her dad still lives in Manhattan, and Stacey visits him a lot), freaked out when she was diagnosed with diabetes. She's an only child, and they were really overprotective at first. But by now they've come to understand that Stacey has a very mature attitude toward her disease. She works hard at keeping herself as healthy as possible. That's where the strength I mentioned comes in. It can't be easy to avoid eating sweets all the time (just think, no Ring-Dings!) not to mention the insulin injections Stacey has to give herself every single day. I have a lot of respect for Stacey.

The newest member of the BSC is Abby Stevenson. She and her twin sister Anna (an awesome musician, who is not in the BSC) moved to Stoneybrook with their mom only recently. Their dad died in a car wreck when the twins were nine. Abby doesn't talk about him much. Abby has dark, thick, curly hair. She wears contacts sometimes (especially when she's playing sports) and glasses other times. She's an excellent athlete, even though she has asthma and allergies which can make it hard for her to breathe sometimes.

My portrait of Abby? It would have to have an energetic feeling, and lots of bright, strong colors (Abby has an independent, vibrant personality!), but it would also reveal some sadness, which I see in Abby's eyes.

Abby is our alternate officer, a job that used to be held by Dawn. "Alternate" means that she has to be ready to take over for any other officer who can't make it to a meeting. That doesn't happen too often, although Abby did just have her big chance to run the club while Kristy was away on a family vacation in Hawaii. She tried hard, but nobody can really replace Kristy.

Now, all the members I've mentioned so far are thirteen and in the eighth grade, like me. But the BSC also has two younger members (we call them junior officers) who are eleven and in the sixth grade. Both of them are extremely responsible sitters, even though they can't sit at night except for their own families. But they take lots of afternoon jobs.

Jessi Ramsey and Mallory Pike are their names, and they are best friends. In fact, they stick together so much that I'd probably keep them together in my abstract portrait. Jessi's part of the picture would combine grace and power. She's an awesome ballet dancer who works out every day and has the muscles and the skill to show for it. She's African-American, with long legs and gorgeous dark eyes, and she comes from a very close family: there are her younger sister, Becca, a baby brother called Squirt, her parents, and an aunt who lives with them.

Mal's family is also close, but it's much, much bigger. Her part of the picture would have to show a quiet space (Mal, who loves to read and write) surrounded by movement and noise (representing her seven brothers and sisters!). Mal has reddish-brown hair and freckles, and she wears both glasses and braces, which she hates.

We also have two associate members: Logan Bruno and Shannon Kilbourne. They take up slack when we're extra-busy, but they aren't required to attend meetings or pay dues. Logan (who is also Mary Anne's boyfriend) is a great sitter. He has a killer smile, blondish-brown hair, and a slight southern accent (he's from Louisville, Kentucky).

Shannon has curly blonde hair, blue eyes, and high cheekbones. She goes to a private school called Stoneybrook Day School, where she's in the Honor Society and a million other clubs. Even so, she usually finds time to sit when we need her.

Although they weren't at the meeting, I thought about the abstract portraits that I would make for Logan and Shannon. Shannon's would be a collage of busy images depicting her activities and achievements. Logan's portrait would be fun and whimsical to show his sense of humor but with swirls of softer colors because he is understanding and sweet.

By the end of that day's meeting I had created an imaginary gallery of portraits. Looking around at my friends made me realize all over again how much they mean to me. The BSC is much more than a club. It's like a family. I'm so glad we're back together. I don't know what I'd do without my friends.

CHAPTER 3

"Okay, people, that's it for today!" Mr. Schubert erased the chalkboard, then stood in front of the class and clapped his hands. "Don't forget to keep up with your homework assignments. We're moving right along here, and if you don't put in the practice, you'll be lost."

Tell me about it. I shut my math book, zipped my protractor into the little pouch in my notebook, and stood up, stretching. Another math class was over. That was something to be thankful for. True, I hadn't understood most of what Mr. Schubert talked about during the past forty minutes, but that was nothing new. As I said, math is a foreign language to me. I don't expect to understand it. I knew I'd make it through the class somehow, though. I always do.

It's not as if I have a learning disability, you know. I've been tested for that. And my I.Q.

is just fine, thank you very much. I am perfectly capable of understanding anything Mr. Schubert or any other teacher throws my way. It's just that I honestly can't see why I should bother. After all, I'm going to be an artist when I grow up, not a research scientist or a mathematician.

There are so many interesting things to think about and look at and *do* in this world. Why waste time on things that don't interest you in the least? For example, angles. And protractors to measure them with. I stuck my math stuff into my backpack and threw the backpack over my shoulder. It was time to head to science class.

"Claudia? Claudia Kishi?" called Mr. Schubert, trying to be heard over the voices of a roomful of kids who were milling around like cattle. I looked up at him, and he gestured to me.

Oh, boy. I've seen that gesture before. The one that says, "Stop by my desk and chat for a second." The one that says, "I'm onto you, and you're heading for serious trouble."

"I have to go — " I began, as I approached Mr. Schubert.

"I realize you don't have much time right now," he said. "Neither do I. I just wanted to let you know that I'm starting to feel concerned about whether you can keep up with the rest of the class."

"Sure, I can," I said. "No problem. I just have to work a little harder." I smiled cheerfully, but inside I was groaning. Work harder on math? I'd just as soon eat brussels sprouts for dessert.

"I'm honestly not sure that will take care of the problem," Mr. Schubert said seriously. "I think you may also need to spend some time brushing up on what you learned in math last year."

"Last year?" I repeated.

"Right," he said. "What you learned last year provides the foundations for what we're doing this year."

"Uh-huh," I mumbled, nodding as I looked down at my shoes (Mary Janes with this cool lug sole and a two-inch heel — they're new and I love them). I couldn't meet his eyes. If I did, he might be able to guess the truth.

The fact is, I don't remember a thing from last year's math class. I know I did the work, and I even understood a lot of what I was doing — at the time. I studied hard for my tests, and then the second I found out I passed I forgot everything. I figured there was no need to clutter my brain with information I didn't need anymore. And who needs it once you've passed the test? Nobody told me I was going to have to remember that material all the way into eighth grade.

"Claudia?" said Mr. Schubert. He looked worried.

I smiled at him. "I'll work on it," I promised.

"Don't forget you can always come to me if you have questions," he said.

Little did he know. It's not just that I have questions; it's that eighth-grade math is one *huge* question. I wouldn't even know where to start. I smiled again. "Thanks," I said. Then I shouldered my backpack. "I'm going to be late," I said, realizing that the kids in the room behind me were all there for Mr. Schubert's third-period class, and that I was supposed to be in *my* third-period class, which is science.

Now, science isn't nearly as bad as math. In fact, there are times when I really like science class. Last year we did these cool experiments. We'd put two different chemicals into a test tube and watch how they reacted. Some would change color, or smoke, or bubble over, while others did nothing at all. I loved the suspense of waiting to see what might happen.

What I didn't love was the part after that, when we were supposed to write up our "research results" and apply something called the scientific method, which I never totally understood. Also, we were supposed to learn all the qualities of liquids and solids and gases, and understand terms such as "density." Some of that I learned, some I didn't. And most of what I did learn, I've already forgotten. Again, I couldn't figure out how any of it would be important to me in real life.

I mean, is somebody going to knock on the door of my art studio some day and ask me the definition of a liquid? And even if someone does, will I care if I can't answer the question? (Only if he's offering a million-dollar prize to everyone who answers correctly!)

I landed in class just in time to hear Ms. Griswold explain that we were going to be identifying rocks that day. She waved toward one of the lab tables and told us that there were a number of specimens on display, and that we were supposed to identify each one as being either "igneous, metamorphic, or sedimentary."

Whew! This was not going to be easy. Those words didn't mean a thing to me, even though I knew Ms. Griswold had gone over them the week before. My classmates and I headed to the lab table, where we clustered around, clutching our notebooks and staring at the rocks. Ms. Griswold had handed out worksheets that we were supposed to fill in.

"I think this one is metamorphic," said Emily Bernstein, picking up a rock with a white crystal thing growing out of one side. I didn't know if it was metamorphic or not, but I did think it had a special kind of beauty. I mean, part of it was just this lumpy old brown rock, and part of it looked like a diamond's cousin. It was a nice contrast.

"Igneous rocks are easy to pick out," said Rick Chow, pointing to a shiny black one. He scribbled something on his worksheet.

I turned over my own worksheet and made a quick sketch of the rock he'd pointed out. It had beautiful depth to it. The color was blacker than black. I wanted to remember what it looked like so I could use that kind of shiny blackness in a painting some day. Was he right that it was igneous? I had no idea.

I did pick out the sedimentary rock, just by luck. I was checking out the gorgeous rust and brown and cream-colored layers in this one huge hunk of stone when I realized Ms. Griswold was standing behind me. "Good, Claudia," she said. "You picked out the best example of a sedimentary rock."

I smiled. I couldn't have cared less what it was called. I just knew it was made up of colors that were so harmonious that only nature could have put them together. That's the kind of blending I aim for in my artwork.

I knew I had a lot to learn about the different

kinds of rocks, but I figured I could study up on it right before our next test. After all, what was the point of trying to memorize all that stuff now? I'd forget it before the test if I did. It was better to wait until the last minute.

At lunch that day, I sat with the other BSC members. Kristy was eating — and dissing — the hot lunch, which was supposed to be chicken chow mein over noodles but looked more like "garbage à la barf," as she put it. I was happy with my Doritos appetizer, my apple, my peanut-butter-and-jelly main entrée, and, most of all, with my dessert: a pack of Starbursts.

Mary Anne had a tuna sandwich she'd brought from home, and Stacey seemed satisfied with her carefully planned meal of a cheese sandwich, an apple, and two Frookies (cookies that are sweetened with fruit juice instead of sugar).

Abby was toying with her hot lunch and looking a little queasy after hearing what Kristy had called it.

Mal and Jessi weren't there, since each grade at SMS eats at a different time.

"You know," said Stacey, who was polishing her apple on her jeans, "I think I'm really going to like math class this year."

Now *I* felt queasy. Stacey is my best friend, and she's fairly normal in every other way.

But I couldn't believe she could just sit there and say such a thing. I raised my eyebrows at her.

"Really!" she insisted. "My teacher is so good. He makes math fun." She grinned at me and took a big bite of her shiny apple.

Oh, please.

"I feel the same way about social studies," said Kristy, putting down her fork. "Ms. Anderson makes it so interesting. I mean, the work is hard, but I don't mind it."

"I know what you mean," chimed in Mary Anne. "It's like the teachers really expect more out of us this year. I mean, in seventh grade we had a fair amount of homework, but this year you really have to keep up. It's kind of cool. They're treating us more like adults, instead of like kids."

"Exactly!" said Abby, beaming.

Great. If being treated like an adult means having tons of homework assigned every night, I'll take the Peter Pan route and avoid growing up. I couldn't believe what I was hearing. My friends really seemed to be enjoying their time in this torture chamber we call SMS. I felt a twinge of nervousness. Was I the only one who was having a hard time keeping up? It sure sounded that way.

It was a big relief to head for art class after lunch. Art class is the bright spot in my school day. It's the one place I feel at home. My attention never wanders when I'm there. I love the art room, with all its special sights and smells. It's lined with closets just bursting with raw materials: clay, drawing pads and pencils, tubes of paint. There are easels set up around the room, and drawing tables, and two pot-ter's wheels. Student artwork decorates every square inch of the walls. Mr. Wong, my art teacher, is always coming up with great ideas for projects, and he never hesitates if someone wants to mix up, say, a huge batch of papier-mâché. "Go to it!" he'll say. "That's what this room is for. Remember, you can't make art without making a mess."

I like his philosophy.

As I walked in the door, I glanced at a flier taped to the bulletin board and my heart skipped a beat. I read through it quickly, hardly believing my eyes. Serena McKay, who is only one of the best artists in the country, was going to be teaching a class at Stoney-brook Community College. A "master class," it was called, for "accomplished amateur art-ists." You had to apply for it by sending in samples of your work, and only fifteen people would be accepted. It would be an intensive class that met for just a few weeks. The idea was to learn how to prepare a piece of artwork for a show. At the end of the class, the student work would be hung in the college gallery, and judges would award prizes, just like in a real art show.

"You should definitely apply," said Mr. Wong, when he saw me reading the flier.

"But it's *college!*" I said. "I'll never get in."

"You never know unless you try," said Mr. Wong.

Now, how could I argue with that?

CHAPTER 4

Thursday

Imagine being stuck inside on these beautiful crisp fall days. Then imagine being sick and being stuck inside — in bed — with no friends to keep you company. And with nothing to eat except runny mashed potatoes and weird gray meat. That's what being in the hospital is like. It seems like anything we can do to make those kids feel better would be really worthwhile. . . .

"Kristy! This is a pleasant surprise. What are you doing here?" Dr. Johanssen waved her clipboard at Kristy. She was dressed in a white lab coat and wore a stethoscope around her neck.

"I'm here to visit Jackie Rodowsky," said Kristy. "Actually, it's kind of a sitting job. His mom likes him to have company as often as possible, and she can't always be here in the afternoons."

On Thursday afternoon, while I was home agonizing over my application for that special art class, Kristy was at Stoneybrook Hospital. She would have gone to visit Jackie anyway, even if it weren't a paid job, because she felt really guilty about his being in the hospital in the first place.

Not that it was actually her fault.

To understand, first you have to know that the BSC has a pet nickname for Jackie Rodowsky. We call him the Walking Disaster. Jackie is a freckled, red-headed, seven-year-old with a nose for trouble. When he's around, life is never boring. Things happen. Oh, boy, do they happen. Vases break, knees are bumped, curtains come tumbling down. Never a dull moment!

Anyway, shortly before the BSC broke up, Kristy was sitting for Jackie. He was in a wild mood, and wasn't listening to her. No matter what she said, he kept misbehaving. He didn't listen when she said he wasn't allowed to climb the tree in the backyard, and while she was occupied with his brother Archie he climbed it anyway. Guess what? He fell out of the tree, of course. Fortunately, he wasn't hurt too badly. That's not what landed him in the hospital.

What happened was this: Jackie's fall out of the tree ended up being the last straw, in Kristy's mind. She felt as if the accident were her fault somehow. And since it was the last in a string of bad things that had happened in the BSC, she figured it was time for the club to break up.

Now, the BSC breakup didn't really have that much to do with Jackie Rodowsky, but somehow he came to believe that it was all his fault. He worried and worried about it, and finally he decided to ride his bike over to Kristy's (which is quite a trip) and apologize.

Unfortunately, he didn't tell his parents where he was going. Even worse, he didn't wear a helmet. And when his bike swerved and hit a tree, Jackie was badly hurt. He was knocked out, and when he came to, he was in the hospital with a lot of concerned doctors looking him over.

Luckily, Jackie's going to be fine. I guess

he's a tough little kid. But a head injury like that could have been very serious. As it is, he's been in the hospital for quite awhile, since the wound still needs attention and the doctors want to be absolutely sure that he's okay.

"I know Jackie will be thrilled to see you," Dr. Johanssen told Kristy, as they walked down the corridor together. "He keeps saying how bored he is. It's not easy for an active kid like him to be forced to stay in bed."

Dr. Johanssen knows a lot about kids. For one thing, she's a pediatrician. For another, she's a mom. Her daughter Charlotte, who's nine, is one of the BSC's favorite sitting charges.

"Will he be able to go home soon?" Kristy asked hopefully.

"Very soon," said Dr. Johanssen. "I'm not handling his case, but from what I hear he should be back to normal in the near future."

"That's great," said Kristy.

"Have fun with Jackie," Dr. Johanssen told Kristy, as they parted near the nurses' desk in the pediatrics wing. "Tell him to stay out of trouble," she added.

Kristy laughed. Telling Jackie to stay out of trouble is like telling a dog not to chase cats. She walked down the hall, grinning. Now that she knew Jackie was really going to be okay, Kristy felt a lot better.

"Knock, knock!" she called, as she peered into Jackie's room.

"Kristy!" Jackie shouted. "All right!" He sat up so quickly that he upset the checkerboard that sat on his bed. A blond boy of about eight was sitting in a chair next to Jackie's bed. They'd been in the middle of a game. The blond boy didn't look ill, and neither did Jackie — except for the big white bandage wound like a turban around his head.

"Shh, shh," said Kristy, a little alarmed. "Take it easy." She gestured around. "This is a hospital. There are sick kids in here, you know."

"I know, I know," said Jackie, rolling his eyes. "They're all friends of mine now. This is John Andru, by the way."

"Hi, John," said Kristy. "How are you?"

"Bored!" exclaimed John. "This dumb old hospital is the boringest place I have ever been in. I can't wait to go home." He folded his arms across his chest.

Kristy didn't know what to say. She couldn't blame John for being bored. Any kid would be. She wondered why John was in the hospital.

"I had appendicitis," he said, as if he knew what she was thinking. "It happened in the middle of the night. I got this wicked bad stomachache — ooh, it hurt so much!" He

35

held his stomach, remembering. "I had to wake up my mom and dad, and when they brought me here the doctors said I had to have an operation right away, or else I might die!"

"Cool, huh?" Jackie asked Kristy. "Want to see his scar? It's awesome."

John was already starting to pull up his shirt. "Uh, no, that's okay," said Kristy, who — surprisingly — has sort of a weak stomach when it comes to huge scars and blood and stuff like that. "Tell me about your other new friends, Jackie," she suggested.

"We can go see them, if you want," said Jackie. "I have to go in my wheelchair, but you can push me."

"Gladly," said Kristy. "But don't you want to finish your checkers game first?"

"That's about the five-hundredth game we've played today," said Jackie, rolling his eyes. "I think we've had enough checkers for awhile."

"Definitely," John agreed.

"Okay, then, let's go," said Kristy, coming around to the side of Jackie's bed with the wheelchair. "Need some help climbing into this thing?"

"I'm fine," Jackie insisted. "I don't know why they don't just let me walk everywhere. My legs work perfectly."

"I guess they're being extra careful," said

Kristy, watching anxiously as Jackie moved out of bed and into the wheelchair. Then they took off, Kristy pushing the wheelchair and John (who said he no longer had to ride in one) walking alongside.

"Turn in here," Jackie commanded, as Kristy was about to pass the room next to Jackie's. "Hey, Jessica, wake up!" he called.

A round-faced girl of about nine sat up in her bed. "I wasn't sleeping," she said. "I was just lying here thinking about potato chips, and pretzels, and tacos. . . ."

"All the stuff you can't eat," said Jackie, sympathetically. "Poor you. All you can have is ice cream and Jell-O and pudding." He grinned. "You don't know how lucky you have it! I'd switch with you in a minute."

"You wouldn't say that if you could feel how sore my throat is," said Jessica. "It's no fun having your tonsils out."

Jackie introduced Kristy, who offered to come back and read to Jessica for awhile after she'd visited with Jackie. "I know it's not the same as tacos," she said, "but maybe it'll take your mind off your throat." She had a feeling that Jessica's food cravings were caused more by boredom and loneliness than by hunger.

Next, Kristy and Jackie and John visited Ashley, who was seven and had just been diagnosed with diabetes. Kristy knew just how complicated Ashley's life was going to be from then on. But she was also able to tell her about Stacey and how diabetes doesn't have to mean the end of a normal life. Ashley looked small and scared in her hospital bed, and Kristy did her best to cheer her up.

After that, Jackie and John brought Kristy to Ian's room. Kristy told me later that Ian seemed like an older version of Jackie. He was a spunky, spirited ten-year-old who had had more than his share of accidents. "I've already broken my right arm, my left big toe, and my collarbone!" he told Kristy, proudly. This time he was in the hospital with a broken leg.

"Just like you," Kristy told me later, reminding me (as if I needed help remembering) of the time I'd been stuck in Stoneybrook Hospital for a whole week. I'd broken my leg badly, and not only did I have to have a cast, but I had to be in traction, as well. That's when they rig up this pulley thing to your leg and hoist it up in the air. It's not comfortable, I can tell you.

While I was in the hospital I had plenty of time to think. And worry. I began to wonder if baby-sitting was such a smart thing for me to do. After all, what if I'd broken my arm instead of my leg, and ended up unable to draw or paint or sculpt? As it turned out, I decided that baby-sitting was worth it, but I never want to have to spend a week in the hospital again.

Anyway, Kristy spent the afternoon hanging out with Jackie and his new friends, and by the end of her day at Stoneybrook Hospital she had come up with a really good idea.

It was simple. The kids in the hospital were bored and lonely. They needed distractions, and they needed to feel as if somebody cared about them. Meanwhile, Kristy and the rest of us in the BSC know lots of kids the same age as those in the hospital, kids who share the same interests in sports and movies and pets and games. Kids who would love to know they were helping to make a sick kid's day a little happier. Why not pair them up? The kids we sit for could write letters, create cards, and in general make sure that the kids in the hospital knew someone was thinking of them.

That's how Hospital Buddies was born. Kristy even came up with the name that afternoon, and that wasn't all. She asked for — and received — permission to start the program right away. It looked as if Kristy was back on track with her great ideas.

CHAPTER 5

"This is me! I mean — this is her. I mean, I'm her. Um, Claudia Kishi here!" I can never remember what it is you're supposed to say when you answer the phone and somebody asks for you. My mother has told me more than once, but I always forget. Then I sound like a jerk when I answer the phone and somebody says, "Claudia Kishi, please."

I was so busy trying to remember what to say that I barely listened to the woman when she said who was calling.

"This is Sandra Katz. I'm with the art department at Stoneybrook Community College."

"This is she!" I blurted out, having finally remembered the correct phrase. "I mean — what? You're calling from the college?"

"That's right," said the woman on the other end, and I swear I could hear a smile in her voice. "I have some good news for you, Claudia."

I sucked in a breath. Could it be?

"You've been accepted into Serena McKay's master class. She was extremely impressed with the level of your work."

"No way!" I burst out. "I mean — you're kidding! I mean — really? *Really?*"

"It's true," replied Sandra Katz with a little laugh.

I couldn't believe it. I'd sent in the abstract self-portrait I'd been working on, but not for one second did I believe I'd actually be accepted into the class. I'd really only applied because Mr. Wong said I should. "Wow," I said. "Cool. I mean — that's great! That's the best news I've heard in a long time."

"Classes will be on Tuesdays and Thursdays, at six," said Sandra Katz. "Be sure to be on time. Ms. McKay wants to make every minute count."

Thursday. This was Monday, so that was only a few days away. I felt a flutter in my stomach; butterflies. Then, suddenly, the butterflies turned to lead. I realized that I hadn't told my parents a thing about this class. I hadn't mentioned applying for it. And I hadn't asked for permission to take it. I thought about all the trouble I'd been having in school. My parents knew I was having a hard time keeping up. There was no way they were going to let me take Serena McKay's class.

"I — " I started to tell Sandra Katz I wouldn't be able to take the class. But the thought of turning down a once-in-a-lifetime chance was too awful. "I'm not exactly sure if I'll be able to take the class," I said, instead. "I'll have to let you know."

"Oh!" she said, sounding surprised. "Is there a problem with scheduling?" She seemed genuinely concerned.

"No, it's just that I have to check with my parents," I explained. "I haven't cleared it with them. Yet." I didn't want to tell her I hadn't even told them about it.

"Well, I certainly hope you'll be able to attend," said Sandra Katz. "Ms. McKay did seem eager to have you in the class."

I felt that fluttering again. Serena McKay wanted *me*! "I'll let you know," I promised. I hung up and paced around the kitchen. How was I going to convince my parents to let me take this class? I wanted to study with Serena McKay more than I'd wanted anything in a long, long time. In fact, the last time I remembered wanting something so badly was when I was almost six and had my heart set on owning Singing Susie, this doll that had a tiny tape recorder hidden in her belly. I'd seen her on TV, and for some reason I felt that I just *had* to have her. Unfortunately, my parents had a rule against buying "junk" that was sold on TV. Still, I had to have Singing Susie. I begged and pleaded and pleaded and begged. I promised to clean my room, to do all my chores, to be good forever.

Finally, my parents knuckled under and gave me Singing Susie for my birthday. I think I played with her for about a day, and then I went back to my crayons and watercolors. And, to be honest, I didn't keep my promise. My room is a mess, my mom still has to nag me about my chores, and I wasn't good forever. Maybe for five minutes, maybe for a whole day, but definitely not forever.

Oh, well.

I was just a little kid then. Now I'm a mature teenager. Maybe I could make a promise I could follow through on. I thought about it, and came up with a terrific idea. I had a math quiz the next day, and Mr. Schubert had said it was an important one. In fact, he'd had one of those little after-class talks with me, during which he told me that failing this quiz would have "major consequences" for me. I wasn't sure what he'd meant by that, but it hadn't sounded good.

I'd been meaning to study for the test, but now I had even more motivation. Suppose I studied really, really hard and did really, really well on the quiz? I could bring it home to show my parents as evidence of my intentions to work harder in school.

Would it work? It had to. No way was I going to miss out on taking Serena McKay's course.

I decided not to waste any time, so I grabbed a glass of milk and headed upstairs. Then I sat at my desk and went through an entire bag of Milky Way miniatures as I studied for the quiz. I studied nonstop until the BSC meeting, and then studied some more after my friends had left. (I didn't say a thing to anyone about the quiz or about Serena McKay's class. I didn't want to jinx myself.)

Not everything I read made complete sense to me. And even though I worked through all the problems at the end of the chapter, I wasn't sure I'd done every one of them right. Still, by the time I closed my math book — late that night, long after a break for dinner — I felt pretty sure that I could ace that silly little quiz. In fact, I could hardly wait for math class the next day.

Well, math class came soon enough, and so did the quiz. I did my best on it, but I had a sinking feeling that all that studying hadn't done much good. Fifteen minutes before class was over, Mr. Schubert told us to finish up. I scratched out one last wild guess of an answer to the final question.

"Okay, people, pass your paper to the person on your right," said Mr. Schubert. He strolled up and down the aisles, taking papers from kids who didn't have anybody on their right and delivering them to kids on the other side of the room.

I passed my paper to Rick Chow, giving him a pleading look as I did. Mia Pappas passed her paper to me. Then Mr. Schubert started going over the quiz, discussing each question and giving its correct answer. I checked Mia's paper carefully, and noticed that almost all of her answers were correct. But every time I snuck a peek over at Rick, I saw him making big red "X's" on my paper. When we finished, Mr. Schubert told us to count the wrong answers and put a grade on the top of the paper. I gave Mia a ninety-two. I craned my neck, but I couldn't see what Rick had given me.

I found out, though. Mr. Schubert gave me that gesture again as class was ending, and when I stopped at his desk he held up my paper. It had a big red forty-five on it. I stood stock still and stared at it. I felt like crying.

I think Mr. Schubert knew it, too. He spoke very nicely to me. "Claudia, did you study for this test?"

I nodded, but I couldn't speak.

"I see," he said. "Well then, what that tells me is that you really don't understand the material. I'm going to recommend — no, I'm going to *require* — that you find a tutor and do some catching up."

I nodded again. I was already thinking that my plan to impress my parents was ruined. How would I ever convince them now? No way could I even mention the math quiz.

"I'm going to send this quiz home with you, along with a note. I want your parents to sign the quiz so I can be sure they understand what's happening here. All right?" He peered up at me.

That did it. A couple of tears squeezed out, before I could stop them.

"It's okay, Claudia," Mr. Schubert said gently. "I'm sure you'll do fine as soon as you have a little extra help." He had no idea that my life had just been ruined.

I nodded one last time, took the quiz and the note, and ran out the door.

That night, after dinner, I showed my parents the quiz and the note and we had a long family conference about my problems in math. I also broke down and told them about the trouble I was having keeping up in my other subjects. I thought they'd be mad, but I think they saw how upset I was. So instead of being mad, they were just sad — which was even worse, in a way.

"Oh, honey," said my mother, patting my hand. "I had no idea you were having such a hard time in school."

"We'll find you a good tutor," said my dad, patting my other hand. (I was sitting between them on the couch.)

Janine reached over and patted my foot (she was sitting on the rug). "There's a girl in my physics class who's looking for tutoring jobs," she offered. "Her name's Rosa. I think you might like her, and she'd be a very competent tutor."

"I know you can catch up if you put your mind to it," added my mom supportively.

I hoped she was right. I was beginning to wonder. Meanwhile, I still wanted to take that art class. "Listen, there's something I need to ask you," I began, crossing my fingers.

They listened carefully to everything I told them. And I think they both felt proud when I told them about Serena McKay's opinion of my work. But neither of them seemed to think it was a good idea for me to take the class.

I felt like I was six years old again, begging for Singing Susie. "This class means so much to me," I pleaded. "And I won't have another chance like this anytime soon. Please?"

Dad and Mom exchanged a look. I could see

that they wanted to say yes. "It just seems that the last thing you need right now is anything that will distract you from your schoolwork," said Mom.

I had a sudden flash — a great idea. "How about if we see it as a *motivation* instead of as a distraction?" I asked. "I want to take this class more than anything. How about this? I'll make a promise to you. If you let me take Serena McKay's class, I'll do anything it takes to bring my grades up. Anything!" I meant every word I was saying, and I think my parents knew it. They exchanged another look, and after a few endless seconds I saw my mother give my father a tiny nod.

I knew, even before she spoke, that the answer was yes.

CHAPTER 6

"Milky Way?" I asked. "Or do you prefer Snickers?" I rummaged around in the bottom of my desk drawer.

"I'm fine, thanks," said Rosa. "Really. I had an apple before I came over."

I thought about explaining my theory that chocolate is an important part of everyone's daily diet, but decided against it. Rosa looked like the type who might come back at me with a full-scale lecture on the Nutritional Needs of the Average Adolescent.

Rosa, as I'm sure you've figured out, is my tutor. My parents don't waste any time, that's for sure. Once they'd heard I needed a tutor, that was it. After our family meeting, Mom called Janine's classmate and set up a tutoring session for the very next afternoon.

Janine had come home in time to be there when Rosa arrived and to make introductions. She and Rosa seemed to be two of a kind, even though Rosa is a little older. She's an actual college freshman. As Janine showed Rosa where to hang her jacket, they made what I could only guess were physics jokes, using words like "inertia," and "mechanical advantage." They cracked themselves up, but I didn't even giggle. I felt as if I came from a different planet.

Not that Rosa is some brainy nerd. She's cool. She even knows a thing or two about how to dress. That first day, she was wearing overalls, Doc Martens, and a funky black newsboy cap, turned sideways. Her black hair is cropped short and she has that "waif" look, with big dark eyes and pale skin.

Anyway, there we were up in my room. I'd been stalling as long as I could, but that offer of a candy bar seemed to be the last dodge I could come up with, and Rosa knew it.

"I think we should start," she said softly, giving me an "I-know-what-you're-up-to" look.

"Okay," I said meekly, remembering the promise I'd made to my parents.

"First of all, I'll have to assess your needs. Which subject do you feel you need the most help in?" Rosa leaned toward me and looked me straight in the eye.

I gulped. "Um, math?" I said. "I just failed a test."

"Okay," said Rosa, writing something in a little book she'd pulled out of her backpack. "And what about science? Are you keeping up?"

"Not really," I confessed.

She made another note.

"Social studies?" she asked gently.

I shook my head. "I'm a little behind," I answered.

"What about English?"

Suddenly, I almost felt like crying. I couldn't look at Rosa.

"Having a little trouble there too, huh?" she asked sympathetically.

I nodded.

"It's okay, Claudia, don't worry," said Rosa. "We'll work really hard and you'll be caught up before you know it." She smiled at me encouragingly.

I wanted to believe her. "You don't know how far behind I am," I said.

"Why don't you tell me about it, subject by subject." She pulled my math book off the top of the pile. "So, where are you, and where are you supposed to be?" she asked, flipping the book open.

We went through each subject, discussing the problems I'm having. She looked over my last math test (without commenting on that forty-five, thankfully!), checked out my social studies notes, and read through an essay I'd written for English. I'd left my science notebook at school, in my locker, but I explained to her about how hard it was for me to remember the different kinds of rocks.

She kept making little notes in her book, and murmuring sympathetic comments as I explained how lost I felt in every subject. Finally, we finished going over my situation. I leaned back and heaved a huge sigh. Then I helped myself to a Milky Way bar. I offered one to Rosa, too, but she shook her head. She was looking over the notes she'd made.

"So, how does it look?" I asked, a little anxiously. "Will the patient survive?" I smiled, to show her I was joking.

She didn't smile back.

"Claudia," she said. "We have some serious work to do. But I think we can put you back on track." She glanced again at the notes she'd made. "It's obvious to me that you're very intelligent."

"Really?" I asked. It felt great to hear that. I know I'm not dumb, but lately I haven't exactly been feeling brilliant.

"Really," she repeated, meeting my eyes with a serious look. "However, you are lazy, scholastically speaking. And sloppy. And you have terrible study habits, and no idea of how to go about learning the basics and then remembering them. You're smart enough to skate along for awhile, but you're going to take a big fall one of these days if you don't buckle down."

"I — I don't usually fail tests," I said in a small voice.

"No, I bet you usually pass them, but not by much. And then you immediately forget everything you just learned. Am I right?"

I couldn't deny it. She was onto me.

"I used to be the same way," admitted Rosa. "Believe it or not."

"I definitely don't believe that. Janine told me you're the best student in her class!"

"I do all right in school," said Rosa. "But it doesn't come naturally to me. I've had to work very hard. But it's worth it, to do well."

Would it be worth it to me? I wasn't sure. I glanced around my room, looking at some of my more recent art projects. A still life of fruit, done in oil paints. A sculpture of a cat. A watercolor of my mother's garden. A necklace I'd made out of bottle caps and wooden beads that I'd painted with acrylics. All of those things had taken a lot of work, a lot of concentration. But I'd done it gladly, because, for me, art is always worth it. I didn't know if I could ever come to feel the same way about math, or English.

Rosa and I worked hard that afternoon,

tackling my math homework. We went over every single problem, and she was incredibly patient. Unlike Janine or Stacey, she explained things to me in a way I could understand. She showed me a new way to check my work so I wouldn't make careless mistakes, and taught me a great trick for remembering the names of the different kinds of angles.

By the time Rosa left, I felt as if I really might be able to handle whatever Mr. Schubert threw my way. I even planned to ask him if I could take that quiz over again, in the hope of bringing my grade up.

I was grateful that Rosa left at a little after five, before any of my BSC friends showed up. I wasn't sure if I was ready to tell them about all the problems I'd been having in school, and it might be awkward to introduce them to my tutor.

As it was, she left in plenty of time. I even had a few minutes to put away my school-books and pull out the goodies I'd saved for our meeting: a big box of Milk Duds, a bag of Sour Patch Kids, and, for Stacey and whoever else was in the mood, some nacho cheese-flavored popcorn.

Then, I opened a drawer and pulled out something I'd received in the mail just the day before. I looked down at it and smiled. Today was the day. I wanted to forget about all my troubles in school. I wanted to pretend that everything was fine. I wanted my friends to see me as the fun-loving, happy Claudia they knew and loved. If this didn't do the trick, nothing would!

I heard the front door slam, and then the unmistakable sound of Kristy thumping up the stairs. Quickly, I shoved the tiny box into my pocket. I'd wait until everyone was there.

"Hey, Kristy," I said, as she came in.

"How's it going?" she asked me.

"Great," I answered honestly. I did feel pretty good about things. First of all, being accepted into Serena McKay's class had been a real boost. (I'd already told all my friends about that. They were thrilled for me.) And secondly, Rosa was a terrific tutor. I had a feeling that if she couldn't help me catch up in school, nobody could.

Stacey arrived next (looking sophisticated-yet-casual in a khaki skirt with a white blouse), and Mary Anne walked in right behind her. Abby arrived next, still glowing from her soccer practice, and last but not least were Mal and Jessi.

I checked my digital clock. It was only 5:27. For once, everybody was early. Perfect! I passed the Milk Duds to Mary Anne, the Sour

Patch Kids to Jessi, and the popcorn to Stacey. "Back in a second," I said, walking out the door. I headed for the bathroom and prepared my surprise. Then I sauntered back into my room.

Kristy, leaning back in the director's chair, was just starting to call the meeting to order. "I hereby — whoa!" she exclaimed, almost falling over when she caught sight of me. Then the others looked up and saw me.

Everybody reacted at once.

"Claudia, I don't believe it!" cried Stacey. "A nose ring?"

"You're crazy," said Abby.

"Your parents are going to *kill* you," said Jessi, shaking her head.

"I think it looks cool," declared Mal.

"What happens when you have a cold?" Mary Anne asked, with a worried look on her face.

"Claudia," said Kristy firmly. "Have you lost your mind?"

I cracked up. Just the reaction I'd been hoping for. "Nope!" I said. Then I reached up and pulled off the nose ring. "It's not as if I pierced my nose," I explained. "It's a clip-on. A fake. I ordered it from a magazine. I thought it would be a great addition to whatever costume I wear to the Halloween dance."

"Oh, my lord!" said Stacey. She cracked up, and the others did, too. Then I had to pass the nose ring around (I wiped it off carefully) for everyone to look at more closely. Meanwhile, Kristy declared the meeting brought to order, and the phone began to ring.

My plan had worked. I'd distracted my friends — and myself.

Then, between phone calls, Mary Anne spoke up. "Claudia," she began, putting her hand on my shoulder. "What's really going on with you? I've noticed that you seem kind of upset lately. And now the nose ring trick. I have a feeling you're trying to run away from something."

Trust Mary Anne to pick up on how I really felt.

As soon as she said that, the floodgates opened. I started to sniff, and then the tears began to fall for real. I confessed everything.

Why had I even tried to hide my troubles? My friends are the greatest. Not only did they promise to support me in every way possible, but they even agreed to make sure my babysitting load was light over the next few weeks, so that I could put all my energy into my schoolwork and my art class.

"No way do we want to lose you," said

Kristy, reminding me of the time my parents almost made me quit the BSC because I was doing so poorly in school. "The BSC is behind you one hundred percent!"

With their help — and Rosa's — I had a feeling I could make it.

CHAPTER 7

Seven days later, I wasn't so sure. About making it, that is.

Rosa was great. So were my friends. But school was turning into this gigantic nightmare for me, a nightmare I couldn't wake up from.

It didn't take long for me to realize that my tutoring sessions weren't going to make enough of a difference. In fact, I realized it almost right away, after the BSC meeting that night. I went back to my math homework to check it one more time, and — even though Rosa had helped me through it only hours earlier — none of it made sense to me.

I felt as if I'd entered the Twilight Zone.

One minute it had all been clear to me, and the next I felt as if I'd never seen a number before in my life. Scary? You bet.

As I'd promised, I worked hard with Rosa and at school. But mostly I tried not to think about my academic problems. Instead, I focused on my new art class, which was turning out to be incredible.

The first night, I was nervous. I was so nervous, in fact, that I showed up fifteen minutes early. I'd spent the afternoon putting together my supplies, making sure that I'd have everything I could possibly need. Then I'd changed my clothes about a dozen times, trying to come up with the perfect outfit. I wanted something that said "very creative," but also said "serious artist." I mean, this wasn't the time for one of my silly theme outfits, like my tropical look or the cowgirl motif.

Finally, I'd thrown on a black sweatshirt with the neck cut out of it, black jeans (doesn't black just say "artist" to you?), and — as a lighthearted touch — my purple high-tops with the orange laces.

When I arrived, I thought the room was empty. I strolled around, checking things out. The class was meeting in an old science lab that had been set up with easels and drawing tables. I looked for the easel with the best placement, found a good one, and set down the red plastic tackle box I use to carry my art supplies.

"Welcome," said someone behind me. I whirled around and saw Serena McKay herself standing there. She looked just like her picture, which had been printed on the flier I'd seen. She was medium height, with long wavy brown hair in a simple style. She was smiling, and her clear blue eyes looked straight into mine.

"I — I — " I couldn't seem to talk.

"You must be Claudia Kishi," she said. "I really liked the self-portrait you sent in. Terrific work."

"Thanks," I said, finally managing to spit out an actual word.

"I hope you'll like the class," she continued. "I think you will."

I nodded. Just then, some other students arrived, and she gave me one last smile and turned to greet them. I went to work unpacking my tackle box. I'm sure I looked serious and professional, but inside I was singing. "Terrific work, terrific work, she thinks I do terrific work!"

I glanced around as the other students took up the easels near me, and my nervousness returned. I was the youngest person in the class. All the other students were, basically, adults. Some were younger adults — college students, I guessed — but many of them were my parents' age, if not older. And they all looked like serious artists. One guy even had a little goatee and was wearing a beret.

Anyway, the point of all of this is that once

class started — and I mean the *minute* it started — I was fine. My nervousness disappeared without a trace, never to return. Serena McKay has this very direct, straightforward style of teaching, and I responded to it immediately. She gave us an assignment right away, and as we worked she walked around the room talking about line and form and composition and texture and all the other things that go into creating a piece of art that lives and breathes and has meaning.

She commented on every person's style, including remarks on their strengths and weaknesses. And everything she said made sense. Right away, I knew she was the best teacher I'd ever had, in any subject.

I guess you know what happens when you have a really good teacher, a teacher you respect. You want to do your best for her, right? So you pull out all the stops and give it everything you have. That's what I did for Serena McKay. And let me tell you, it felt great.

It felt great to be good at something. Great to know that I understood what the teacher was talking about, and that I could respond with work that proved it.

It was, like, the opposite of school.

I worked for hours with Rosa, every single day after school. And I did all my homework, every night. But even with all that effort, I was still falling further behind every day.

In math class, Mr. Schubert said he'd noticed an improvement but that I still didn't seem to grasp the basics.

In science, Ms. Griswold told me I'd need to go back and review before I'd be able to understand the concepts she was teaching.

Mr. Blake, my social studies teacher, said he appreciated my effort but that I'd have to pick up the pace on my reading.

And Mrs. Hall, who is my English teacher, told me I'd better start spending some time in the resource room.

Which I did. As if it weren't enough to be spending all that time on homework and tutoring sessions, now I was heading for the resource room during lunch hours and study halls. The aide there, Mr. Matthews, was helpful. But he seemed to agree with everyone else: it was up to me to work harder, to review, to keep up.

I felt as if I were on a treadmill, and somebody kept turning up the speed. One night, working with Rosa, I would feel as if I finally understood what we were doing in science class, but then the next day Ms. Griswold would be shooting ahead to some new area I'd never even heard of.

It was hopeless.

If it hadn't been for Serena McKay's class,

I don't know what I would have done. But her class kept me sane, and gave me something to look forward to.

Finally, on Thursday, everything came to a head. Once again, it was all because of a math test. This time I did a little better. Instead of forty-five I received a fifty-eight. But that wasn't enough to impress Mr. Schubert, since it was still a failing grade. This time, he didn't bother sending a note home with my parents. Instead, they received a phone call just before dinner that night. A phone call from Mr. Kingbridge.

Mr. Kingbridge is the assistant principal at SMS. He's not a bad guy. In fact, he's pretty nice. But if there's trouble, he's on the scene. He's the one who hands out punishments, suspends people, even expels them. (Not that I've ever heard of a student being expelled from SMS. But it could happen.)

Why was he calling my parents?

To "invite" them to a meeting, with him and Mrs. Amer, the guidance counselor. The meeting would take place the next afternoon, and I'd have to be there, too. I'd rather have had a date with Dracula.

I figured I was going to have to hear yet another lecture. I figured my parents would be upset, and that I'd have to promise to do better (even though I couldn't imagine what else I could possibly do). I figured it would be embarrassing, mortifying, and possibly even humiliating. And it was. But what actually happened was even worse than I ever could have imagined.

Here's the scene: My parents are sitting on the couch in Mr. Kingbridge's office, wearing their work clothes and looking very concerned. I'm seated nearby, in a plastic chair. I'm looking concerned, too. I'm wearing a black wool jumper over my favorite red turtleneck. Mrs. Amer, also wearing a concerned look, plus a tasteful but boring pale yellow suit, is sitting in a chair next to Mr. Kingbridge's desk. And a concerned-looking Mr. Kingbridge, dressed as usual in a horrifically ugly brown suit paired with a tie that looked as if he'd spilled spaghetti sauce all over it, sits behind his desk, hands folded as if he's praying.

Did I mention that we all looked concerned? We did.

Now that the scene is set, how about some dialogue? (I'm trying to make this as dramatic as possible.)

Mrs. Amer started things off by introducing herself to my parents. Everybody exchanged "pleased-to-meet-you"s. Then Mr. Kingbridge (whom they've already met) began to talk about the trouble I'd been having, in all my subjects. He listed every single late homework assignment, every missed problem, and every failed pop quiz.

Humiliating? You bet.

But not surprising, to me or even to my parents. After all, they'd watched me struggle all fall. They know it's been hard for me.

Then Mrs. Amer began to talk.

"Claudia," she said. "I don't know if you've thought about whether or not you want to go to college someday."

"College?" I asked. "Um — " To tell the truth, that seemed a long, long way off.

"Or even art school," Mrs. Amer continued. "Either way, it's not too early to be thinking about it. You'll have to do well in high school in order to be accepted at any college or art school, and in order to do well in high school you have to do well in junior high."

"That's right," Mr. Kingbridge put in. "And in order to do well in eighth grade, you have to do well in sixth and seventh."

"All of that makes sense," said my mother. "But what are you saying? Claudia's been working very hard. We've even hired a tutor."

"I know," said Mrs. Amer. "But clearly, it's not enough. Claudia is falling further and further behind. She is lacking the foundations that should be helping her learn eighth-grade material. At this point, she may not be able

66

to catch up, no matter what she does."

I gulped. I knew she was right. That was exactly what I'd started to think.

"So what do we do about it?" asked my father. He put his hand on my shoulder.

"We take drastic measures," said Mrs. Amer. She turned so that she was looking straight into my eyes. "Claudia," she began. "You're going to have to repeat seventh grade. You'll start on Monday."

CHAPTER 8

Saturday

Kristy, if you're reading
this (and I know you
are), I have to hand
it to you: once again
you've come up with a
Really Good Idea.
The kids had a ball
with the Hospital
Buddies project.

Abby's right. Even if I did have to end
up spending the afternoon with my not-so-
dearly beloved siblings. And even if the Pike
kitchen table never recovers from that huge
glue-and-glitter spill. . .

"They're all yours!" said Mal that cold, rainy Saturday afternoon, as she greeted Abby at the Pikes' front door. Mal was on her way out to sit for Marilyn and Carolyn Arnold, identical nine-year-old twins who are regular BSC clients, while Abby was on her way *in* to sit for Mal's sisters and brothers.

"Great," said Abby. "Can't wait." She loves baby-sitting for the Pikes, since there are so many of them. She thinks it's a blast.

"And I can't wait to leave!" said Mal, as she put on her jacket. "They're driving me up the wall." She grinned. "Jordan's your official helper today, by the way."

Jordan is one of three identical triplets (the other two are named Adam and Byron). At ten, they are the next-oldest kids in the Pike family, and not only are they old enough not to need sitters anymore, but they're old enough to help out. (We used to send two sitters to the Pikes, but not anymore.)

"Excellent," said Abby. "Where is everybody, anyway?" She cocked her head to listen for the sound of thundering Pikes.

"In the den," replied Mal. "Arguing about Halloween costumes," she added, before Abby could ask what they were doing. She

69

opened the front door. "Have fun," she sang out, as she left.

Abby headed for the den, and as she neared that room she began to hear the sounds of a major sibling squabble. When she opened the door, it hit her full force.

"You can't be a pirate," Byron was yelling at Adam. "*I'm* going to be a pirate!"

"I'll be whatever I want," Adam yelled back, folding his arms in front of his chest.

"I'm going to be a mummy," declared Nicky, who's eight. "I already bought all the bandages."

"You're going to look so dumb," sneered Jordan. "Nobody's even going to know what you are."

Nicky looked as if he were about to burst into tears.

"I'll be a hippie girl, living in a hippie world," Vanessa chanted loudly. She's nine, and wants to be a poet someday. She tries to speak in rhyme whenever possible.

"I'm being Pocahontas," claimed Margo. She's seven. She kicked up her feet to show that she was wearing moccasins. "I already have the shoes."

"No!" shrieked Claire, who's the youngest Pike, at five. "Nofe air! Nofe air!" (That's her standard cry when she believes life is treating her badly. Translated, it means "no fair.") "I was going to be Pocahontas. Mommy already bought me the wig!" She reached between the sofa cushions and dredged up something that Abby said later looked like a hairy black mat.

Abby sighed. Halloween was approaching fast, and the excitement of it seemed to be dividing the Pike family. She could see that it wasn't going to be a nice, quiet, relaxing afternoon.

Abby stepped into the room, whistled through her fingers, and then held up her hands in a "T." "Time out, you guys," she called loudly.

Everybody quieted down and turned to look at her. The silence lasted for about a count of three. Then they all started to complain to Abby about their siblings.

"Adam stole my costume idea!" Byron bawled.

"Jordan said I was going to look dumb," whined Nicky.

"Claire can't be Pocahontas," yelled Margo. "I'm the only Pocahontas in this family!"

"Whoa, whoa," said Abby. "Hold on. Let's see if we can figure this all out in a civilized way." She made the kids sit down. "First of all, why don't all three of you guys" — she pointed at Adam, Byron, and Jordan — "be pirates. You can be a whole pirate crew. After all, pirates usually travel in groups, right?"

They looked at each other warily.

"Maybe," said Byron. "But I want to be the one who has a parrot on his shoulder."

Adam sat up, as if he were about to argue, but Abby shushed him. "You can work out the details later," she said. "Now, Nicky. You need to work on some ideas to make that mummy costume really convincing. Have you thought about fake blood, for example? A little bit goes a long way."

Nicky looked interested.

Jordan nodded. "That would help," he said. "But he won't do it right. He'll just make a mess."

"Maybe not, if you help him," Abby said pointedly.

"Why should I — " Jordan began, but Abby gave him a Look and he sat back.

"Vanessa," Abby went on. "A hippie costume sounds perfect for you. I have some tie-dyed stuff you could borrow."

"Vanessa is a hippie, Vanessa is a hippie," chanted Nicky, under his breath.

"So?" asked Vanessa, staring him down. "Hippies are cool, mummies are fools."

Nicky glared at her. But Abby changed the subject before he could come up with a snappy comeback. "Claire," she said, "How about being a *different* Native American? You could be Sacajawea, for example. She's just as cool as Pocahontas, if not cooler."

"Saca-wacka-*who*?" asked Claire.

"Sacajawea," Abby repeated. "She helped to guide Lewis and Clark, the famous explorers."

"Okay," said Claire agreeably.

Abby heaved a sigh of relief. Maybe the bickering was over. But no sooner did she relax than it started up again.

"Mom said I could go trick-or-treating with you guys this year," Nicky told the triplets.

"What?" "No way!" "Are you kidding?" The triplets exploded.

"We're going with our friends," said Jordan.

"Not with any little brothers," added Adam.

"Or sisters," put in Byron, making a face at Margo.

Nicky had that "I'm-about-to-cry" face on again, and now Margo wore it, too. "Why does Claire get to be Sacajawea?" she wailed. "I want to be Sacajawea. Every girl in my class is going to be Pocahontas."

Abby rolled her eyes. There was just no way she could win. Then, suddenly, like a bolt from the blue, she thought of something. "If you can't beat 'em, distract 'em," she told me later. "It never fails."

"Hey, guys," she said. "How about if we

forget about Halloween? I have a great project for us to work on."

That caught their interest.

Abby explained about the idea for Hospital Buddies. "You guys all miss Jackie, right?" she said. "Well, just think how lonely he must feel, missing all his friends at once. But what if he got a really neat card, or an interesting letter in the mail? Don't you think that would help him feel better?" She went on to tell the Pikes about some of the other kids Kristy had met in the hospital, and about Kristy's idea for Hospital Buddies. "Every one of those kids is probably as lonely and bored as you can imagine," she finished. "How about if we see what we can do about changing that?"

"Okay," said the kids.

"Can we call some friends and ask them to come over to make cards and write letters?" asked Jordan.

"We'll help with everything," offered Byron.

"Okay, sure," agreed Abby. As long as the kids were occupied and not fighting, she didn't mind a few more. "Why not?"

"I'll make some calls," offered Adam.

"I'll find the art supplies," said Vanessa. "Crayons, pencils, paste, and glue, we'll send wonderful cards to you!" She ran off, spouting poetry.

Claire, Margo, and Nicky helped set up the kitchen by covering the table with newspaper and bringing in extra chairs. Jordan and Byron took charge of mixing up some lemonade and putting out graham crackers for everyone.

By the time the room was ready, the doorbell began to ring. First to show up was James Hobart, whose family is Australian. James is eight, and in the same class as Nicky. "Hey, mates," he said, as he came in, shaking off raindrops.

Next, Shea Rodowsky — Jackie's nine-year-old brother — arrived. "This is the greatest idea," he said. "Jackie is really tired of being in the hospital."

Finally, Carolyn and Marilyn Arnold showed up, with Mal in tow. Mal and Abby smiled at each other.

"Couldn't escape that easily," Abby said, laughing.

"I'm baaa-aack," sang Mal. She shrugged. "Oh, well," she said, peering into the kitchen. "At least they're not fighting anymore."

That was the truth. As soon as the kids started working on the project, their differences were forgotten. Abby said later that she knew all along that their problem was boredom. After all, on a rainy day kids do tend to become crabby, and who can blame them? But now the warm, bright kitchen was full of happy, busy kids.

They cut and pasted, painted and glued. They wrote letters about what they'd been doing in — and out of — school. They drew pictures of what they were going to be for Halloween (Abby wondered if they'd start arguing again at that point, but they didn't.) Vanessa wrote a beautiful poem about autumn, and Margo illustrated it. Shea wrote a story for Jackie, all about a boy who fell on his head and turned into a monster. (Mal helped him with the spelling; Shea's dyslexic.)

By the end of the day, the kids had produced a whole grocery bag full of Hospital Buddy stuff. They'd also produced a huge mess, including that glue-and-glitter spill Mal mentioned. But, as promised, the triplets helped with cleanup. Abby said she'd drop the cards and letters off that very evening. Hospital Buddies was a success.

CHAPTER 9

"Hey, Stace, how's it going?" I smiled at Stacey as I passed her in the hall.

She ignored me. Just walked by, as if I weren't there.

"Stacey?" I asked. I turned and followed her. She was wearing a short plaid kilt, a white baby-T, black tights, and black, chunky-heeled shoes. "Nice outfit," I said. I'd never seen it before. She must have gone shopping since I'd seen her last.

She didn't answer, didn't turn around.

"Well, okay," I said, shrugging. "Be that way." I felt like a jerk following her down the hall, so I turned and headed back toward science class. Ms. Griswold was standing near the door, talking to another teacher and greeting students as they passed into her room.

"Hi, Ms. Griswold," I said. "I remembered my book today, see?" I held it up, smiling. She's always giving me a hard time about forgetting to bring my book to class.

She didn't smile back. She didn't say a thing. In fact, she looked right through me.

"Ms. Griswold?" I said. My voice came out sounding quavery. Why was everybody ignoring me? Just then, Rick Chow walked by. I reached out and grabbed his jacket. "Rick!" I said.

He pulled away from me, brushing at me as if I were a bothersome insect. He didn't seem to hear me — or see me.

That's when I figured it out.

I was invisible.

Nobody at SMS could see me.

"Hey, Claudia!" Somebody called my name, and I whirled around to see who it was.

"Ron?" I asked, bewildered. Why could Ron Belkis see me when nobody else could?

"That's my name, don't wear it out," he said, with a silly grin. Ron has always had a little crush on me. Usually I just ignore him, mainly because he's a seventh-grader and I can't stand immature boys.

Suddenly, something clicked. Seventh-grader! *That's* why Ron could see me, and why Stacey and Rick and Ms. Griswold couldn't. All those people were from my eighth-grade world, the place in which I no longer belonged. And Ron? He was from my new world, my seventh-grade world.

"Oh, no!" I moaned. "No! I can't stand it!" How could I go through life being invisible to my best friends? I imagined a BSC meeting: I'd be sitting on my bed, trying to catch Kristy's attention, but she would look straight through me, just the way Ms. Griswold had. "What a nightmare!" I moaned.

That's exactly what it was. A nightmare.

My alarm went off then and I rolled over, still moaning a little. I pulled my hands out from under the covers and looked at them. Perfectly visible. I gave a sigh of relief.

Then I remembered.

While it was true that I'd just woken up from an awful nightmare, and that I wasn't invisible, the fact remained that my life was going to be very different, starting that morning. It was Monday, and from now on I was officially a seventh-grader.

I'd been trying hard not to think about it all weekend. I'd told my friends, of course, but other than that I hadn't talked about it much. Everyone tried to make me feel better about it, but I still felt miserable. After all, there was no escaping the truth.

I'd been kicked out of eighth grade. How humiliating.

I rolled out of bed and pulled on the clothes I'd laid out the night before. It had taken some thought to figure out what to wear on my first day back in seventh grade. I didn't want to draw too much attention to myself; then again I didn't want to blend in too much, either. It's important to me to be an individual, no matter what.

After a lot of indecision, I'd settled on my moss-green Gap jeans, paired with a rust-colored cardigan I'd found at the vintage clothing store. Also, my new Mary Janes, and a moss-green scrunchie so I could tie up my hair in a Pebbles Flintstone ponytail on top of my head.

I pulled on the clothes and checked once more in the mirror. "Good enough for seventh grade," I muttered. Then I headed downstairs to face what turned out to be one of the longest, hardest days of my life.

I arrived in the kitchen to find that my dad had woken up extra early, just to make me blueberry pancakes, normally my favorite breakfast. I choked one down so he wouldn't feel bad, but the truth was that I had absolutely no appetite.

My parents and Janine kept up a bright chatter at the breakfast table, as if nothing had changed. As if my whole life weren't going in reverse. I could barely keep myself from shouting at them to stop it, but I restrained my feelings. I knew they were only trying to make me feel better.

Finally, I grabbed my backpack and left for school. Mom gave me a hug as she saw me out the door, and Janine and my dad both wished me luck.

I walked to school alone that day, which was the way I wanted it. Usually I walk with a bunch of BSC friends, but somehow I'd known I wouldn't be able to stand that this morning. It would be awkward for everyone, and there was no point in putting my friends through that. Besides, I just felt like being alone with my thoughts.

By the time I arrived at school, I thought I felt ready for whatever the day would bring. My first stop was at Mr. Kingbridge's office, where I picked up my new schedule. I checked it over quickly. Usually, looking over a new schedule is fun. You check for good teachers, compare notes with friends to see who's in your classes, all that. This time, it wasn't fun at all. I noticed that I'd have two of my teachers from the year before: Mr. Peters, who teaches seventh-grade math, and Mr. Redmont, who teaches social studies. I'd still have Mr. Wong for art, for which I was thankful. My English teacher would be Ms. Chiavetta, who was new at SMS, and my science teacher would be Ms. Spacey. I'd heard the kids make fun of her name, but other than that I knew nothing about her.

I'd also received a new locker and combination. I guess Mr. Kingbridge felt that it would be better if my locker were situated in the same hall as the other seventh-graders'. It felt terrible to pass by the hall where my old locker was, to look down it and see Stacey and Kristy chatting and laughing as they gathered their books for the morning. And it felt even worse to stand alone, dialing in a new, strange combination and listening to the chatter of seventh-graders all around me.

That morning they were talking about some kid who had made a smart remark to Mr. Redmond the week before. They were speculating about how he was going to be in a lot of trouble if he didn't shape up. They sounded so naive. That kid would be fine. If they wanted to know what *real* trouble was, they could ask me.

I glanced at my new classmates, noticing that they looked a lot more than one year younger than my eighth-grade friends. The boys, especially, looked as if they were about nine years old. And most of the girls were dressed in babyish fashions I'd given up when I was ten.

My first class was math. My most hated subject *would* come first. I walked in with a group of kids, trying to blend in. But it was no use. Mr. Peters spotted me right away.

"Claudia!" he said, beaming. "Welcome ba — " he stopped himself. "I mean, welcome! It's wonderful to see you."

I nodded and tried to smile. It was sweet of him to act so nice, especially since I hadn't been one of his best pupils. He pointed out an empty seat in the front row, and I sat down, very aware that my classmates must be staring at me. I tossed my head and pulled out a notebook, pretending not to care.

I did care, though. I cared a lot. I cared about other kids thinking I was dumb. I cared about whether they were laughing at me. And I cared about the fact that I was sitting there in a class full of strangers, while down the hall my old math class, full of people I'd known since kindergarten, was going on as usual.

I tried to concentrate on what Mr. Peters was saying. He was talking about how to make a bar graph, which was one of the few things I was ever good at in math. I think it had to do with the fact that they often come out looking like some kind of cubist drawing.

Eventually, math class was over. As if on automatic pilot, I moved through the rest of my day. In social studies, Mr. Redmont made a point of being friendly to me. He even made sure to introduce me to everyone in the class, *without* making it obvious that I'd been demoted from eighth grade. (Not that everybody didn't already know. Believe me, news travels fast in a small school like SMS.) Science wasn't too bad. Ms. Spacey turned out to be nothing like her name, and I liked my lab partner, a boy named Josh Peterson. And Ms. Chiavetta seemed like a good English teacher.

Still, I felt like an alien creature. The worst part was lunch. Since each grade eats at a different time, I didn't have one single friend in the cafeteria. I ate lunch alone, which was *not* a fun experience. Somehow the Yodels I'd brought tasted like cardboard, and not even the Fluffernutter sandwich my mom had let me bring (for a special treat) could make me happy.

All in all, it was a miserable day. I felt just about as invisible as I had in my nightmare.

That afternoon at our BSC meeting, my friends tried to cheer me up, but I was too bummed out. Eventually they gave up and started talking about all the usual stuff. Like how much homework they'd been given that day, and why Mr. Fiske always wears such ugly ties, and how Shawna Riverson could possibly think that purple eyeshadow is attractive. All eighth-grade gossip. Mal and Jessi didn't seem to mind listening, but I sure did. Every word reminded me that I was out of the loop.

The only good part of the day came that

night, after dinner. I was up in my room attacking my math homework (and studying for a quiz) when I suddenly realized that I actually understood what I was doing. Awesome! At that moment, my phone rang. It was Stacey, "just checking in" to see how I was feeling. Excitedly, I told her about the graph I was making. She was nice and supportive, and I didn't feel as if she were looking down at me in the least.

Maybe, just maybe, as Stacey pointed out, there was a silver lining to seventh grade after all.

CHAPTER 10

Tuesday

Jackie's back! Isn't it great?

It's excellent. He doesn't seem quite up to his old Walking Disaster form, but I'm sure that'll come.

No question about it. Meanwhile, all the other kids seem to be taking up the slack. . . .

I forgot to mention one other thing that happened at our BSC meeting on Monday night. Mrs. Rodowsky called to let us know that Jackie had come home from the hospital that weekend. They'd kept the news quiet at first, since they wanted Jackie to have a calm first few days at home. But now he was feeling fine and ready to return to normal life, which included going to school, seeing friends, and doing just about anything he wanted — as long as he didn't *over*do.

Mary Anne was the one who took the call, and after she hung up she was quiet for awhile. Then, just as the meeting was breaking up, she made an announcement. "I think we should have a welcome home party for Jackie," she said. "Just a small one. We don't want to overwhelm him. And nothing too fancy. In fact, I think a spontaneous party would be best. I'm going to call some kids and see if they can come over to my barn tomorrow afternoon."

"That sounds great!" said Kristy. I could tell she wished she'd thought of it. "But I can't come," she continued. "I have to sit for David Michael."

"Bring him!" said Mary Anne.

"I'm sitting for Matt and Haley Braddock," said Abby. "Can I bring them, too?"

"Definitely," Mary Anne replied.

Mary Anne arranged everything with Mrs. Rodowsky, who suggested that the party *not* be a surprise, since "that might be a bit too much excitement for Jackie." Then Mary Anne made a few more phone calls and rounded up a group of kids. Some were Jackie's teammates from the Krushers, the softball team Kristy coaches (Matt, David Michael, Jake Kuhn, Nicky and Margo Pike, Buddy Barrett). Some were just friends (Charlotte Johanssen, Jessi's sister Becca, and the Arnold twins). All the kids were excited about helping to welcome Jackie home.

The next day, right after school, Nicky and Margo showed up early at Mary Anne's. "We want to help decorate," Nicky announced, holding up a tattered roll of red crepe paper. "This is left over from my birthday party."

"And I brought some napkins," added Margo, showing Mary Anne a stack of brightly colored napkins. "They're left over from *my* birthday party."

"Wonderful," said Mary Anne. "I'm just finishing up a banner. Want to help?" She led them to a table in the back of the barn, where she'd laid out an old bedsheet. Painted on it in huge purple letters were the words JACKIE'S BACK!

"Cool," said Nicky.

"Let's put some stars and stuff on there, too," said Margo, reaching eagerly for a paint-brush — and, in the process, knocking over the pot of yellow paint. "Ooops," she said. "Sorry!"

That was the first accident.

"No problem," said Mary Anne. "If you moosh the paint around a little and make some rays coming out, I bet you can make a sun out of that spill. Why don't you try? I'm going to go check on the snacks."

Mary Anne was pouring ginger ale into the punch bowl when Kristy and David Michael arrived. "Look what we brought!" said David Michael, holding up a round grayish object.

"Nice," said Mary Anne, looking a little puzzled. She added some grape juice to the punch and stirred.

"It's a softball from an important Krushers game," explained Kristy. "We're going to have all the Krushers at the party sign it. And later we'll have the rest of the team sign it, too. But we'll present it to Jackie today."

"It's a real honor to have your team give you a signed ball," said David Michael. He tossed the ball into the air and caught it, tossed it and caught it, tossed it and — dropped it into the punch bowl.

That was the second accident.

"Yow!" he cried. "Uh-oh."

"Um, no problem," said Mary Anne, using the ladle to fish it out. "A little softball flavoring never hurt anyone." She handed the ball, now tinged a sickly pink, back to David Michael. Then she turned to greet Matt and Haley Braddock, who had just arrived with Abby.

"Hi, Matt," she said, smiling and waving. "Hi, Haley."

Matt smiled back and gestured with his hands.

"Hi! He says it was a great idea to have this party," translated Haley. Matt, who's seven, is profoundly deaf and communicates with American Sign Language. He's also excellent at reading lips. Haley, who's nine, does a lot of interpreting for Matt. They're great kids.

"My mom helped me make these," Haley continued, holding out a plate full of Rice Krispies treats.

"Yum!" said Mary Anne, taking the plate. "Thanks a lot! Hey, how about if you guys go check on Nicky and Margo? I bet that banner's just about ready to hang up."

"I'll give them a hand," offered Abby.

The third, fourth, fifth, sixth, and seventh accidents happened as the group hanging the banner took a tumble off the bench they were standing on. Except for a banged knee (Abby), and a bruised elbow (Matt), nobody was hurt.

They just stood there and laughed, after they'd dusted themselves off. Then they climbed back onto the bench and hung the banner, which looked terrific. (Mary Anne told me later that it wasn't nearly as good as one I would have made, but that it was "very colorful.")

Soon the Arnold twins arrived, and so did Charlotte and Becca. Jake Kuhn, who's eight, was the last to show up — before Jackie, that is. He came with his baseball glove. Jake's always ready for a game of catch.

Accident number eight happened when Nicky and Jake started tossing a softball around. One of Jake's throws went wild and shattered a small window.

"Oh, no!" cried Jake. "I'll help fix it tomorrow. I know how, since I've broken a bunch of windows at my own house." He was blushing.

"It's okay, Jake," Mary Anne reassured him. "But I think that's enough indoor softball for today." She shook her head. "If this is what happens *before* the Walking Disaster arrives," she said to Abby and Kristy, "I'm not sure I want to be here for the rest of the party."

The banner was hung. The crepe paper was dangling from the rafters. The napkins were piled, ready for use. Then, just as Mary Anne was putting the finishing touches on the snack table, Jackie arrived.

"Yea!" shouted the kids, rushing to greet him.

"Easy," cautioned Shea, who had come with his little brother.

"That's okay," said Jackie, reaching out for high-fives and hugs. "I'm not made out of glass."

But, Mary Anne told me later, he *did* look somewhat fragile. His face wasn't as ruddy as usual; even his freckles looked faded. And his manner was subdued. This Jackie Rodowsky was not the rough-and-tumble kid we all knew and loved. This Jackie was a little more careful, a little slower in his movements, a little quieter.

As the kids thronged around the snack table, Mary Anne, Abby, and Kristy exchanged worried looks. "He's still recovering," whispered Kristy. "He'll be himself again soon, I'll bet."

"Meanwhile, at least we don't have to worry about any more accidents," Mary Anne whispered back.

"I wouldn't be so sure," said Abby, gesturing toward the group of kids. Nicky had just drenched himel with punch. A Rice Krispies treat had found its way into Margo's hair. And the plate of brownies was balanced precariously on the corner of the table.

"This is perfect for a party for Jackie!" cried Kristy. "The whole *party* is a Walking Disaster."

Finally, the food was gone and all the kids had been cleaned up. Mary Anne asked Jackie — who'd been sitting in the honorary spot at the head of the table — what he'd like to do next.

"Could I say something?" asked Jackie.

"Absolutely," said Mary Anne.

He turned to face his friends, and began his speech a little shyly. "Well, first of all I just want to tell you how cool it was to have those letters and cards you sent. All the kids in the hospital really, really appreciated it."

"Hooray for Hospital Buddies!" yelled Margo.

"The other thing I wanted to say is this," continued Jackie, gathering steam. "I'm never, *ever* going to ride my bike without a helmet again." He looked around at all his friends. "And if I ever see one of you riding without a helmet, you're going to be in big trouble."

After that, the party went into full swing. The kids played hide-and-seek (always great in Mary Anne's barn) and freeze tag until they were exhausted. Then they sat down for some more punch, and started to talk about Halloween.

Nicky told everyone how Jordan had helped

him put together the "scariest mummy" costume ever.

Charlotte reported that she was going to be a doctor, and that her mom was letting her borrow a white lab coat and a real stethoscope.

Matt was planning to be a baseball player, and so was Jake Kuhn. They decided to trick-or-treat together.

"Too bad the kids at the hospital can't trick-or-treat," said Jackie.

"Oh, man," groaned Nicky. "I never even thought of that. That's *awful!*"

Everyone was upset by the thought of such a tragedy — being in the hospital for Halloween ranks right up there with having the measles on your birthday.

Then, suddenly, Carolyn came up with a terrific idea. "Why don't we each split our trick-or-treat candy with a hospital buddy? That way they won't miss all the fun."

Kristy latched onto the idea and expanded it. By the time the party ended, the kids had planned everything, including a Halloween party in the children's ward (Kristy was sure she could get permission). The kids in the hospital were going to love it, and so were our charges.

Jackie — and all the other kids — went home happy that evening. The party had been a real success, despite the Walking Disaster theme.

CHAPTER 11

I hate to admit it, but I think I've learned something from the experience I'm going through. Here's the thing: no matter how bad something seems at first, you can usually find some good in it. Also, things are often not as terrible as they first look.

Mature, huh?

That's me, Claudia Kishi. The most mature seventh-grader on the face of the earth.

Sounds sickening, but it's true. The fact is that by Tuesday afternoon I was feeling a whole lot better about being back in seventh grade. For one thing, I was starting to get used to the idea, and so was everybody else. For another, I was discovering that there were some real benefits to being older than everybody else in my classes. Namely: I had suddenly become sort of a mini-celebrity.

Let's face it. Seventh-graders can be fairly dorky. There wasn't one person in that whole grade who even approached the level of coolness I've attained — and they all knew it.

The first thing I noticed Tuesday morning was that about ten seventh-grade girls came to school wearing their hair in Pebbles ponytails, just like the one I'd worn on Monday. One of them even asked me where I'd bought the scrunchie I'd been wearing. (When I told her I'd made it, she looked so impressed I thought she was going to faint.)

Next, I discovered that I'd never have to eat lunch alone again. Kids were shoving each other aside in their rush to find a spot at my table. The girls wanted to talk about clothes and hairstyles. The boys didn't talk much at all; they just kind of stared at me. I wondered if some of them were trying to work up the nerve to ask me out.

In the halls, between classes, I was always surrounded by a bunch of kids. My entourage and I would pass Stacey or Kristy and I'd wave to her.

What a hoot!

Also, I was actually doing well in every single one of my classes. In science class I even went so far as to raise my hand when Ms. Spacey asked a question — and when she called on me and I gave the answer, it turned out to be right. I nearly passed out. I'm not sure if Ms. Spacey realized she was part of a historic occasion.

Next, I *really* impressed Ms. Spacey by predicting that adding one chemical to another would make the first one turn from red to blue. Then I impressed myself by writing up the lab results in my notebook.

In social studies, I felt on top of my reading for the first time in a long time. Not only that, but I was beginning to remember some of the things I'd learned the year before about the American Revolution. This time I wouldn't forget them as soon as I passed the test, either. I understood now that it was important to learn things for keeps, not just for tests.

And in English, Ms. Chiavetta told me in front of the whole class that I'd structured my paragraphs "beautifully" in the essay I'd written after my first day in her class. (True, she did mention to me afterward that my spelling and punctuation needed work, but hey, I can't change everything overnight.)

Best of all, believe it or not, was math class that morning. I knew we'd be taking a quiz, and I'd studied carefully the night before. Mr. Peters smiled at me as he handed out the question sheets, and I smiled back. Suddenly, math wasn't something to be afraid of. What a great feeling.

I went over the quiz, answering each question in turn and leaving the questions I wasn't sure about for later (a technique Rosa had taught me). Then I went over it again, taking more time with the questions I was unsure of. Finally, I went over it one more time, checking my work to make sure I hadn't made any silly mistakes in addition or subtraction.

When I looked up at the clock, I was shocked to see that there was still plenty of time left in the period. That had to be the first time I'd finished a math test so quickly. I looked around the room and noticed that most of my classmates were still hard at work on their tests. That made me panic. Had I missed a whole bunch of questions? I turned the test over, but the other side was blank. Then I turned it right-side up and checked over my answers again, just in case.

Finally, I sat back in my chair and closed my eyes. I'd earned a little daydreaming time, hadn't I? I thought about my art class. I was still glowing from last Thursday's session.

It had been an excellent class. Serena McKay had things to say about art that I'd never heard before. She talked about the "spirit" of creativity, and told us that, as artists, we had an obligation to ourselves and to the community. An obligation to provide beauty, and an obligation to provoke thought and emotion.

Being called an artist by Serena McKay made me feel incredible.

She also talked about what it means to show your work to the rest of the world. She told us about her first show — and how nervous she was about it — and about other shows she'd had in famous galleries all over the country. She explained how she prepares for a show: everything from how to choose which pieces to exhibit to how to decide what to wear to the opening.

Later, as we worked on the pieces we were preparing to show, Serena stood by my easel. "You have quite an eye, Claudia," she said. "I love this line here, and the way it intersects with this one," she added. "And you use color in marvelous, subtle ways, which is unusual in an artist your age."

I was thrilled. "Thank you," I said quietly. I looked around at the other students after she left. One of them, a woman about my mother's age who was at the easel next to mine, was looking at me. I could tell she'd heard what Serena McKay had said.

"She's right," she said. "Your work is excellent. I've been trying to reach your level for about fifteen years, and I haven't made it there yet." She made a face. Then she shrugged and smiled. "Still, I've had fun trying."

I couldn't believe it. This woman had been

working on her art for longer than I'd been living! And yet, according to her, she wasn't as good as I am.

Needless to say, art class had been a huge ego boost.

"Okay, class," said Mr. Peters, jarring me out of my daydream and back into the very real world of math class. "Let's exchange papers and do some quick correcting. We only have ten minutes before the period is over."

I glanced at my paper one last time before handing it to Tim Ryan, a blond, freckled boy who was sitting next to me. He traded his paper for mine, and I pulled out a red pen.

As Mr. Peters went over the answers, I felt a mounting sense of excitement. I knew I'd done well. Tim, on the other hand, had not. I felt terrible about all the red Xs I was making on his paper, and realized how bad Rick Chow must have felt all those times he had to mark my tests.

Finally, we reached the end of the test. "Quickly now, count up the points and write the grade on top of the test," said Mr. Peters. "Remember, each wrong answer is two points off."

I counted up Tim's Xs, multiplied by two, and subtracted the total from 100. Then, reluctantly, I wrote a sixty-four on the top of his test. If only he'd had one more right answer, he would have passed! Poor Tim.

I was so busy feeling sorry for him that for a second I almost forgot about my own grade. But Tim reminded me. He gave me a thumbs-up and a huge grin as he held up my paper so I could see the number on the top.

Ninety-six!

Little did he know, that was one of the best marks I'd ever received on a math test. And I mean *ever*. Even back in fourth grade, when I had a patient teacher named Ms. Jameson, I never did so well on a test.

I felt so great I could hardly sit still. Fortunately, the bell rang then and I was able to jump up and grab my test from Tim's desk. I wanted to kiss that ninety-six, but I stopped just in time. I wouldn't have wanted my lip gloss to blur that stupendous number. Instead, after I'd showed my grade to a smiling Mr. Peters so he could record it, I filed the test away in my notebook. I could hardly wait to show it to my parents that night.

I walked out of the classroom feeling as if I were floating on air. If this was what seventh grade was going to be like, I didn't care if I had to stay there until I was thirty!

Then my world came crashing down.

I barely noticed the chattering of the group around me as I strolled along. I did notice, however, a poster for the Halloween dance, which was going to be held on Friday night.

I thought about the costume I was working on. I'd come up with this great punk look, pairing an old leather jacket of my uncle Russ's (he used to have a motorcycle before he was married) with torn fishnet tights, my big black Doc Martens, and a spandex miniskirt. Of course, I'd wear the nose ring. That was an important part of the look. And I was thinking about using one of those temporary dyes to put a purple — or maybe a green — streak in my hair.

I wondered if my mom would let me out of the house.

I stepped forward to take a better look at the poster and to check what time the dance was going to start. That's when I saw something that made my heart lurch.

"Eighth-grade Dance" said a line at the top of the poster.

"Oh, my lord," I murmured to myself. "That can't mean what I think it means, can it?"

Before I knew it I had marched into Mr. Kingbridge's office and asked to see him. Moments later I was sitting in front of his desk. "I can go, can't I?" I asked. "I mean, I know I'm taking seventh-grade classes, but I'm still technically an eighth-grader, right? I mean, in terms of age and maturity and stuff?"

I was babbling. And here's why: as soon as I'd started to speak, Mr. Kingbridge had begun to shake his head. I didn't want to hear him say no, so I just kept talking.

But I couldn't talk forever, and finally I wound down. Mr. Kingbridge looked genuinely sorry as he explained that he really couldn't let me go to the dance. "I'd be setting a precedent if I did that," he said. "And, even though I agree that you have the maturity of an eighth-grader, you are officially a seventh-grader now, Claudia. You're more than welcome to attend the afternoon party for sixth- and seventh-graders, of course." He said that last part gently, as if to soften the blow.

It didn't work. I felt stunned.

In that one second, I forgot everything good about being in seventh grade. That mature Claudia — the one who was able to accept change — disappeared. I realized that from now on I would be separated from my friends. The fact was, they were in eighth grade, and I wasn't. I was kidding myself if I thought I belonged at that dance, but I sure didn't belong at any babyish afternoon party, either.

Suddenly, everything had changed for the worse. How could I ever have convinced myself that being back in seventh grade was going to be okay?

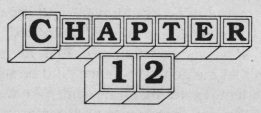

CHAPTER 12

I left school that day feeling as low as I've ever felt. I walked home slowly, shoulders slumped, kicking a rock in front of me. (I knew I was completely ruining the toes of my Mary Janes, but I didn't care.) Fortunately I didn't run into any of my friends. If I had, I would have burst into tears.

Sure, it had been nice to feel that I was doing well in school, and it was cool to know that all the seventh-graders looked up to me. But if I was going to be exiled from the social life I should be having as a thirteen-year-old, what good was any of that? I mean, so what if I'd scored well on a stupid math quiz? And as far as being looked up to, well, I've always been one of the cooler kids in school anyway (not to boast). The way I see it, friends are the most important thing in the world. And if I wasn't going to be allowed to socialize with my friends, I was going to be miserable — even if I was making straight A's in every subject.

I *was* miserable. And nothing could snap me out of it. In fact, I kept feeling more and more miserable as the afternoon wore on. When I walked into the kitchen at home, for example, I saw a bowl full of the treats my mom was planning to give out on Halloween. Since she doesn't believe in junk food, she gives out things like raisins in those little boxes, or plastic baggies full of dried apricots. It's humiliating. She's been doing it for years, and by now we hardly ever have any trick-or-treaters.

Anyway, the thought of Halloween and of trick-or-treating should have cheered me up. I mean, a holiday based on candy? What could be better? But this Halloween, I'd be a social outcast. My friends would be whooping it up at a dance, and I'd be — where? Probably home in my room, feeling sorry for myself.

I grabbed a snack and went upstairs. Unpacking my backpack gave me another reason to feel lousy. There were all my seventh-grade books. I piled them on my desk and gave them a nasty look. I had lost all motivation for schoolwork. "Who cares?" I said out loud, glaring at the math test that had slipped out of my notebook. "Big deal. Ninety-six. So I'm a genius now. A genius with no friends."

Then I saw the nose ring sitting on my dressing table. I wasn't going to have the chance to wear the great costume I'd planned. I felt like crying, or throwing something. It just wasn't fair. It wasn't fair at all.

I thought of calling Stacey to tell her how unfair it all was, but I decided she wouldn't understand. None of my friends would. Suddenly I resented each and every one of them, just because they happened to be in the proper grades for their ages.

But you know what? By seven-thirty that night, I felt a little better. Why? Because I was at Serena McKay's class. Being in a place where I felt as if I truly belonged did wonders for my mood.

That night, Serena reminded us that there was only one more class session. "By the end of Thursday's class, your artwork must be ready to be hung in the gallery. It must be finished and framed and ready to be seen by the public," she said. "I know some of you are nervous about showing your work for the first time. That's normal."

"Whew!" said the man at the easel next to mine. Everybody laughed.

"What I'd like you to do tonight is take some time during class to walk around and look at the work your classmates have been doing," Serena went on. "Introduce yourself, talk about the work, ask questions. This should help you feel more used to the idea of other people looking at — and critiquing — your art."

It was a great class. I spent some time working on my piece (it was almost finished), and then I walked around the classroom checking out the other artists and their work. All of them were older than me, and many of them were even older than my parents. But as I chatted with each one, I discovered that we spoke a common language. They all loved art as much as I do, and that gave us plenty to talk about.

The first woman I met was a veterinarian who paints in her spare time. She was tall and gray-haired and very serious, but she lit up when I told her how much I liked her painting.

Then there was the blonde woman, a single mom who said she loved Serena's class because it was something she did just for herself. And the man with the goatee, who turned out to be very funny, and also very good with pastels. There was a nurse who said she worked on her art from one to three every morning, after she came home from her late shift at the hospital. And a tall, skinny man who said he worked three part-time jobs just so he could afford oil paints and canvas.

What a great group of people! Everybody I talked to that night was friendly and interesting and talented. And you know what? I felt as if I fit right in. Even though I was so much younger, I was one of them; I was accepted. Age didn't matter. This class was so different from SMS, where you're defined by what grade you're in, and where I now felt I didn't belong at all.

Thinking about Serena's class was the only thing that helped me make it through school on Thursday. Every time I felt depressed, or sad, or lonely, I'd think about the fact that there was a place where I was happy and felt at home.

My teachers must have wondered what had happened to the enthusiastic Claudia of the day before. I was staring out of windows, doodling in the margins of my notebook pages, and never, *never* raising my hand to answer a question. After all, I figured seventh grade was probably easy enough that I could pass even if I didn't put in a whole lot of effort.

The seventh-graders were still clamoring to sit at my table for lunch, but I made it clear that I'd just as soon eat alone. And I shot nasty glances at all the Claudia wannabes who were wearing their hair in Pebbles dos and showing off their new Mary Janes.

It wasn't hard to avoid my BSC friends during school, but that afternoon I had no choice. At five-thirty they arrived for our meeting.

The funny thing (funny peculiar, not funny ha-ha) was that nobody even noticed, at least at first, that anything was wrong. I guess they were too excited about the stupid dance and the dumb party they'd be going to on Friday. I don't think they even noticed that I hadn't made much of an effort to provide snacks. All I'd dug up was a bag of stale pretzels, but nobody seemed to care.

The main topic of conversation during that day's meeting was costumes. My friends may be mature, responsible businesswomen but they still love to dress up.

"I found the coolest beaded purse at the Salvation Army store yesterday," Stacey reported. "It's going to be the perfect finishing touch for my flapper outfit."

"That was such a creative idea," Jessi told her. "I can hardly ever think of anything to be, so I usually end up being a ballet dancer."

"Well, you have the clothes for it," said Mal, who was dressing as one of her heroines. "Not like me. I really had to do some searching to find an outfit that Emily Dickinson would have worn."

"My main concern for costumes is that they be comfortable," claimed Abby. "That's why I'm going as a soccer player."

"Mary Anne and Kristy have the best costumes," said Stacey, giggling. "You guys are going to win for best team costume, I bet you anything."

Mary Anne was dressing as Little Red Riding Hood, and Kristy was going as — guess what? — the Wolf. She'd found this horrifically realistic rubber mask somewhere, which is what had given them the idea.

"How about you, Claud?" asked Mary Anne. "Are you still doing the punk thing?"

I mumbled something and shook my head.

"Claudia?" asked Mary Anne.

"I'm not going to the dance," I said.

"Why not?" asked Abby.

"Kingbridge says I can't. Because I'm not in eighth grade anymore."

There was a shocked silence.

"That's awful!" Kristy said finally.

"How unfair!" exclaimed Stacey. "Why didn't you tell me?"

"I just found out yesterday," I said. "Anyway, it's no big deal." I didn't want to talk about it. If I did, I'd just start crying. And even though they were acting as if they cared, my friends probably didn't think it was a big deal, either. After all, I was a seventh-grader now. I didn't really belong in their world.

"Well, you'll come to the afternoon party, then, won't you?" asked Mal. "It's really going to be fun. There'll be games and everything."

"Sure," I answered, just to finish off the conversation. I could barely keep myself from rolling my eyes when I heard about "games." How babyish can you be?

Thankfully, the phone started to ring and I was saved from having to talk about it anymore. Calls were coming in from parents who needed sitters to take their kids trick-or-treating, and Mal and Jessi and I decided to plan a group outing. Since everyone else would be at the dance, it was up to us to cover that night's jobs.

Later, when the meeting was over and everyone was gone, I did cry — just a little. Then I blew my nose and pulled out my homework. I started on my math problems, but my mind kept drifting, so I switched to English and tried to study vocabulary words. I couldn't concentrate on those, either, so I opened my social studies book and read through a whole chapter, without absorbing a word. Finally, I opened my science notebook, took one look at the lab results I was supposed to write up, and snapped it shut.

It wasn't that the work was hard. I just didn't care anymore.

I sat at my desk, feeling sorry for myself. What if I couldn't even cut it in seventh grade? Would Kingbridge send me back to sixth? My mind drifted into a horrible daydream. What if I kept being sent back forever? I pictured myself sitting at one of those little-kid desks in third grade.

The fantasy grew until finally I saw my friends in caps and gowns, happily graduating from high school, while I sat in a circle in Mrs. Kushel's kindergarten room, displaying a crayon drawing for show-and-tell. Claudia Kishi, Teenage Kindergartner. Was that my destiny?

CHAPTER 13

"Come on, everybody, let's bob for apples!" Ms. Spacey, dressed as the Bride of Frankenstein, was acting like a cheerleader at a pep rally. She was just full of the Halloween spirit.

So was everybody else in the cafeteria, everybody except me. Halloween had finally arrived, but I didn't care. I had decided against wearing my costume to school, even though I've always loved to do that. We have a new Halloween tradition at SMS. Everybody wears costumes to school and in the middle of the morning the students meet in the parking lot. We form a parade and head down the street and around the corner to the elementary school, where the teachers have brought the little kids outside for a special recess. We parade around the school playground, waving at the kids and shouting, "Happy Halloween!" They love it, we love it. It's a lot of fun.

Or, at least it usually is. This year it wasn't.

Not for me. Marching along with the others, I felt even more out of place than usual. I was wearing school clothes (jeans, boots, one of my father's white shirts, and a vest) and everybody else was dressed outrageously, even some of the teachers.

There was Mr. Schubert, for example, in a big black cape and fangs: Dracula. And Mrs. Hall was dressed as a gypsy, in a long red skirt and lots of jewelry. They led the parade.

Alan Gray, the most obnoxious boy in school, was marching near me in a Mask costume: green face, yellow suit, and all. Cokie Mason, a BSC archenemy, was dressed all in pink, as Barbie. (Could you gag?) And Ron Belkis, who had been after me to go out with him, was dressed as a knight in not-so-shining (it was made out of cardboard, I think) armor.

My BSC friends were in a bunch near the front of the crowd, but I stayed away. I felt awkward about joining them. They were all in costume, for one thing. And for another, I just didn't feel that I belonged with them. After all, they were either in eighth grade or sixth. I was in the middle, in seventh grade. No man's land. (Or should that be no *girl's* land?)

After the parade, we went back to our classes, but none of the teachers was trying too hard to teach us anything. They knew it was a lost cause. Everybody was way too keyed up about Halloween. To my eye, the seventh-graders were acting like a bunch of children. I mean, Halloween is fun, but come on. It's mainly for little kids. Once you're over ten years old, how much can it mean to you?

A lot, I guess. Judging by the excitement level at the sixth-and-seventh-grade party, which started right after school, some middle school kids still think Halloween is the most important holiday of the year.

When Ms. Spacey invited everyone to bob for apples, for example, the kids thundered over to her like a herd of buffalo. (If you can imagine a herd of buffalo dressed up like characters such as Bart Simpson, Mr. Spock from *Star Trek*, and a werewolf, that is.)

Soon apple-bobbing was in full swing, and I was glad I'd stayed on the other side of the cafeteria. The boys were acting really obnoxious, as only seventh-grade boys can. They were splashing water around and tossing apples at each other. The girls were screeching and squealing and carrying on. What a scene. I rolled my eyes.

"Isn't this great?" asked Jessi, joining me. She was dressed as a sugarplum fairy, all pink and frilly, and she looked terrific. Mal was with her, wearing a high-necked white blouse and a floor-sweeping black skirt. Her hair was powdered white and twisted into a bun. She carried a long feathered quill pen.

They grinned at me. "See, it's fun, right?" Mal asked. She didn't wait for an answer. "And the decorations are awesome, aren't they?"

The "decorations" consisted of a bunch of black and orange crepe-paper streamers, a few corn stalks, and a pile of pumpkins.

"Yeah, sure, they're great," I muttered. Mal gave me a funny look. But before she could say anything, Mr. Peters (who was wearing an Einstein mask, with a funny white wig) announced that it was time for the pumpkin-carving contest.

"Enter it, Claud," said Jessi, giving me a little push. "You'll win first prize for sure."

I stood stock still, resisting the pressure of her hand. "So?" I said.

"So it'll be cool," said Mal. "We can show you off to all our friends. They'll be so impressed when they find out what a great artist you are."

"Oh, please," I said. "Who cares if a bunch of little brats are impressed by me?"

Mal and Jessi just stood there with their mouths open, staring at me. I saw the hurt in their eyes, but it was too late to take back what I'd said. Anyway, I didn't want to take it back.

I meant it. The sixth- and seventh-graders were so immature.

I turned and walked away from Mal and Jessi. As I left the cafeteria, Ron Belkis called after me. "Claudia, my fair maiden, wait up!" The visor on his knight costume kept falling down over his face as he ran after me.

What a jerk. I ignored him and kept on walking. And I didn't stop until I was home. Then I went to my room, shut the door, and did some serious sulking.

Two hours later, when the BSC meeting started, I knew I'd been wrong to take out my feelings on Mal and Jessi. I apologized to them as soon as they arrived, and they seemed to accept my apology. But I knew Mal and Jessi didn't really understand what I was going through. None of my friends possibly could. After all, they were right where they belonged. How could they know how awful it was to feel as if you didn't fit in?

The only place I'd felt at home recently was at Serena McKay's art class, and now that was over. I'd attended the final session the night before. Our work was hung in the art gallery, ready for the show and judging on Saturday. I wasn't even sure I was going to attend the show. I didn't expect to win a prize. After all, I was only an eighth — I mean a *seventh-*

grader. So why go? It would only make me feel more depressed.

Art class was great, but it wasn't real life. I had to face that fact.

Anyway, at the beginning of our meeting, I passed out pretzels again, but again, nobody seemed to notice that the *cuisine* wasn't up to my usual standards. Mal and Jessi were too busy reporting on how much fun the party had been, and the rest of the club members were gabbing about plans for the dance.

"So, my mom said she'd drive us over, and Watson will pick us up," Kristy told Abby. "Is Anna coming?"

"Oh, sure," said Abby. "She's dressing as Hildegarde von Bingen. That's some famous woman composer. Nobody will have any idea who she is, but that doesn't bother Anna."

"Sharon said she'd be glad to give us a ride," Mary Anne told Stacey. She glanced in my direction and sighed. "I sure wish you were coming, Claudia," she said.

I felt tears come to my eyes, but I refused to let them drop. "I don't," I declared. "Who wants to put up with Alan Gray prancing around saying 'Smmmokin!' all night?" I didn't mean to sound sour, but I guess I did. After that, none of my friends even made eye contact with me.

Okay, I admit it. I sulked through the meeting. I was acting like a child, and I knew it, but I couldn't seem to stop. I felt separated from my friends, but the truth was that I had been the one to do the separating. They didn't care what grade I was in. And it wasn't their fault I couldn't go to the dance. They cared about me — or at least, they did until I started acting like the world's biggest pill. Eventually I was going to have to snap out of it, but that day I just couldn't find it in my heart to do it.

If anything could pull me out of my doldrums, you'd think it would be trick-or-treating. After all, what's more fun than being with a bunch of kids on the most kid-oriented holiday of the year? I mean, kids love holidays, but Halloween is something special. There's the dressing up part of it, which would be fun on its own. But then you add in the fact that people are handing out candy right and left, and there you have it. Kid heaven. And Claudia heaven, too — you'd think. Dressing up + kids + candy = happiness, right? Well, not in this case. Somehow I managed to hold onto my lousy mood throughout the evening.

Mal and Jessi and I had agreed to take a bunch of kids trick-or-treating, so we met at Mal's house right after dinner. The Pike kids were already on hand, of course, and they were practically bouncing off the walls with excitement.

Adam, Byron, and Jordan weren't coming with us. They were going trick-or-treating with friends, instead. But they didn't mind showing off their pirate costumes. Jordan nearly took off my head with his sword when I walked into the Pikes' den, and Adam let out a yell of "Avast, ye landlubbers!" Jordan showed me his papier-mâché parrot, which looked excellent perched on his shoulder.

Vanessa drifted in next, dressed in tie-dye, bells, bangles, and beads, and looking very hippie-ish. "Peace and love and happiness," she said, flashing me the peace sign. "Halloween is the grooviest."

Nicky's mummy costume was perfect, and Margo and Claire both looked like authentic Native American girls, though I have to admit I couldn't tell Pocahontas from Sacajawea.

Jessi arrived next, with Becca and Charlotte in tow. Charlotte was dressed as a doctor and looked just like her mom, and Becca was wearing one of Jessi's old tutus. No sooner had the two of them arrived than the rest of the kids showed up.

The youngest were Jenny Prezzioso and Jamie Newton, who are four years old. Both of them have baby sisters, so their parents were happy to have us take the older siblings trick-or-treating. Jamie was a robot, and Jenny was a black kitten. Then there were Laurel and

120

Patsy Kuhn. Their older brother Jake had made plans to go trick-or-treating with Matt Braddock, so the girls came with us. Laurel, who's six, was dressed as a fifties girl in a poodle skirt and saddle shoes. Her sister, who's five, made an adorable fairy princess in a pink satin dress, her mother's high heels, and a "diamond" tiara.

The kids had a terrific time. We took them on a tour of two different neighborhoods, and they filled up their goodie sacks to the brim. (They told everyone about Hospital Buddies, and people were very generous with the treats.) Mal and Jessi (who were also wearing their costumes) collected some treats, too. They thought the night was terrific.

Me? My mood didn't lift. Oh, I chowed down a couple of chocolate bars the kids gave me, but for once candy didn't make my outlook brighter. All I could think about was what a good time every eighth-grader at SMS was having that night while I was stuck with the little kids. It was the worst Halloween ever.

CHAPTER 14

My phone started ringing before I was even fully awake the next morning. The first call was from Stacey.

"Claud? Boy, did I miss you last night!" she began. "The dance was okay, but it just wasn't the same without you." She chattered on, telling me about everyone's costumes, about the decorations, about the refreshments. Every couple of sentences she mentioned again how much she'd missed me, or told me that somebody had asked about me.

I knew she was trying to make me feel better, and I tried to be polite. But the fact was that she was only making me feel worse about missing the dance. It sounded like a pretty good one, and hearing about it made me feel even more left out.

Finally, she asked if she'd see me later at the hospital party. I said yes, but I wasn't so sure about that. I didn't feel much like going to a party.

As soon as Stacey said good-bye and hung up, the phone rang again.

"Claud? It's Mary Anne. I just wanted to tell you how much I missed you last night." Mary Anne was using that understanding, sensitive voice of hers. "Logan said he missed you, too," she went on. Then she told me about the dance.

I listened, saying "Uh huh," and "That sounds like fun," in the right places, but the fact was that I couldn't wait to finish our conversation and say good-bye.

Finally, Mary Anne wound down. I hung up the phone, climbed out of bed, and started thinking about what to wear. Then the phone rang again. This time it was Abby.

"Hey, Claudia!" she said. "Know what? You didn't miss much. The dance was okay, but not great." She went on talking about how much everybody had missed me, but I started to tune out. Obviously, my friends had decided I needed cheering up, and they'd all agreed to call me. Didn't they think I'd see through their plan? They were treating me like a little kid. I hated the idea that everyone felt sorry for me.

By the time Kristy called, I was fed up. I

came close to being rude to her, but she didn't seem to notice. She just went on and on about how lousy the decorations were without me on the committee, and how much everyone had missed seeing what costume I had come up with. Blah, blah, blah. I heard her voice, but I wasn't really listening. Finally, she said she'd see me that afternoon at the hospital party. Then we said good-bye and I hung up my phone with a sigh. Hearing about the dance, I felt like the Poor Little Match Girl, standing on the cold and snowy sidewalk with her nose pressed against a window, looking into the bright warmth of the rich people's house.

I sat on my bed, still dressed in my pajamas, and thought about pulling the covers over my head and hiding from the world for the rest of the day. I certainly didn't feel like going to the Halloween party at the hospital. I wasn't even too thrilled about attending the opening of the art show. I suppose I should have invited my friends to the opening, but I hadn't even mentioned it to them, and nobody had remembered to ask about it. Same with my parents and Janine, who were busy with errands and weekend activities. If I went to the opening, I'd have to go alone.

It was tempting to think about going back to sleep — until I thought of Serena McKay.

She had been so nice to me, and so supportive. After the show, I'd probably never see her again. It wasn't right to stay away. I wanted to see her one last time and thank her for everything.

I forced myself off the bed. I marched over to my closet and pulled out the first thing I put my hands on: a long black jumper with red embroidery around the neckline. I put that on over a white turtleneck, added a pair of dangly earrings with red glass beads, and twisted my hair into a casual knot. "Good enough," I said, checking myself in the mirror. For once, I didn't much care how I looked. All I was going to do was check out the show quickly, congratulate the prize winners, say thanks to Serena McKay, and head back home.

Once the show was over, that was the end of art class. I'd have nothing to look forward to. Just months and months of being a seventh-grader. It was going to be a long, long year.

I ate breakfast by myself, since Janine and my parents had already left the house. Then I threw on a jacket and headed to the college.

On the way, I started to feel a tiny bit excited about seeing my work hung in a real art show. I've had my own art shows (the best one was the junk-food painting show, featuring portraits of Twinkies and Ring-Dings), but this

125

was different. Lots of people who really knew something about art would be coming to this show, including the arts reporter from the *Stoneybrook News*.

I felt even more excited when I arrived at the college and saw a big yellow banner with red letters. It was strung across the main entrance, and it advertised our show. People were streaming in. As I entered the building, I followed the crowd that was heading for the show.

"Hey!" I heard someone call. I turned to see a man from my class, the one with the goatee. He was passing in the opposite direction, across the crowded hall. He gave me a smile and the thumbs-up sign, and I smiled back. The crowd pushed me along, so I didn't stop to talk.

As I entered the gallery, I looked around for Serena McKay. She was nowhere in sight, but I did spot some of the other students from my class. Everyone waved and smiled at me. "There she is!" I heard someone say, as they pointed in my direction. I turned around, expecting to see Serena behind me, but nobody was there.

I decided to take one more look at all the artwork, even though I'd seen it just the other day. Somehow all the drawings and paintings looked different now, when the gallery was fully lit and thronged with people. They looked more official, more like pieces of art in a museum. I started with the paintings hung in the first small room of the gallery, figuring I'd work my way back to where my piece was hung, in the third room.

As I was rounding a corner, I nearly bumped into Dr. Johanssen. "Why, hello, Claudia," she greeted me with a smile.

"Hi, Dr. Johanssen," I said. It was nice to see her there. I hadn't expected to see anyone I knew at the show.

"Congratulations," she said.

"Thanks!" I answered, feeling like a real artist. I wasn't sure what she was congratulating me for, exactly. Maybe that's just what people say to you at openings.

I went on gazing at the artwork in the second room. The room was full of people, all of whom were laughing, talking, and sipping cider from plastic champagne glasses. They moved from painting to painting, looking thoughtfully at each one. It was interesting to hear their comments.

"I like the sense of space in this one," said a man dressed in black to a woman dressed in white.

She nodded. "It has an elegant, almost O'Keeffe-like sensibility," she added, standing back to take a better look.

I rolled my eyes. Just then, I felt a hand on my shoulder.

"Congratulations, Claudia," said one of my classmates, the single mom.

"Thanks," I said. "Congratulations to you, too!"

She gave me a funny smile and moved on, swept by the tide of people.

I made my way through the second room and walked into the third. I spotted Serena McKay talking to a tall man who was trying to juggle a notebook, a pen, and a tape recorder. I figured he must be the arts reporter. I thought I'd avoid interrupting his interview with Serena, so I began to look at the paintings instead, intending to work my way through the room so that my piece was the last one I'd see.

"There she is now," I heard Serena say. "Claudia, Claudia!" she called my name over the hubbub in the room.

I looked up and smiled, and she gestured to me to join her.

"I'm so proud of you," she said, as soon as I was standing next to her. She smiled and gave me a hug. Then she turned back to the reporter. "This is the young student I've been telling you about. Claudia Kishi. That's K-I-S-H-I."

"Right," he said, making some notes.

I was amazed. Why was Serena McKay telling the reporter about me?

"The judges had no idea that they'd awarded the first prize to my youngest student," Serena said to the reporter. "They were shocked when I told them that Claudia is only in eighth grade."

"Seventh," I said automatically. I was still trying to make sense of what she was saying. First prize? I couldn't have heard correctly. I glanced across the room, trying to see my piece. As I looked, a tall man wearing a dark suit stepped aside, and I had a clear view.

A view of my piece — with a blue ribbon fastened to the frame.

I'd won first prize! I couldn't believe it. How could the judges have thought my piece was better than all the rest? I was just a kid compared to the other students.

"Claudia is incredibly talented," Serena McKay was telling the reporter. "I predict she'll be making a name for herself in the next few years."

He nodded and made some more notes. Then he thanked us both, told me that a photographer would be by soon to take my picture for the newspaper, and left.

I was still in shock. Serena McKay just smiled at me. "How about that, Claudia?" she said. "You won. Isn't it wonderful?"

And that's when I lost it. I began to cry.

I was so embarrassed, but Serena McKay didn't seem upset at all. She led me into a small janitor's closet, sat me down on an over-turned bucket, and made me tell her what was wrong.

Everything spilled out. How it felt to have been sent back to seventh grade. How I missed my friends, and felt as if I'd never fit in with them again. How sad I was that art class was over.

She listened, patting my back occasionally and handing me paper towels to blow my nose on. Then she told me something incredible.

"I can relate to what you're feeling, Clau-dia," she said gently. "You know why? Be-cause I was held back myself. Twice. I had to repeat sixth grade, and then I had to repeat ninth grade. I though I'd never finish school."

"But you're so smart!" I cried.

"So are you," she said. "But that doesn't mean we can do well in certain learning en-vironments. Me, I have a learning disability. I still have a hard time reading. But with the encouragement of one excellent art teacher — Polly Thompson — I managed to make it through high school anyway, and I was even accepted at Rhode Island School of Design, one of the best art schools in the East. Now I have a good career teaching art. It took a lot of work and a lot of perseverance, but I made it. And so can you."

I was amazed. "Polly Thompson is one of my favorite artists," I said. "Next to you, that is. That's so cool that she helped you. And now you're helping me in the same way." I sniffed a little, and she handed me one more paper towel.

"Let's go on out there so you can enjoy all the attention a first prize winner deserves," she said. "I have the feeling this is only the beginning of your long and fabulous career."

CHAPTER 15

By the time I left the gallery, I was feeling terrific. It was as if my whole world had brightened. It wasn't just winning first prize that did it, either. It was the talk I'd had with Serena McKay. She understood what I was going through. Not only that, she'd been through it herself, and I could see how well she'd turned out. She was an inspiration.

She and I talked a lot, there in the janitor's closet, and one of the things she said really hit home with me. She talked about having a support group — for her it was her family, plus one or two loyal friends — and about how important it was to feel that people cared about her.

I thought of my friends in the BSC. I'd been so silly to think that it mattered to them what grade I was in. They were my friends, and they loved me no matter what. They'd tried to show me that, but I'd been so busy feeling

132

sorry for myself that I hadn't let myself see it. My BSC friends are my friends forever, and I should have known they'd always be there for me with love and support.

Suddenly, I couldn't wait to see them. As soon as I could, I said good-bye to my art class friends. Then I spent a few minutes talking one last time with Serena McKay. She made me promise to keep in touch, and told me again how much she'd enjoyed having me in class. Then she hugged me, and I hugged her back. I took one last glance at that blue ribbon hanging next to my painting, and then I headed home.

If I hurried, I could still make it to the hospital Halloween party on time. But first, there was something I had to do. Finally, I felt like wearing a costume. Back in my room, I glanced at the clock and realized there wasn't enough time to pull together the punk look I'd planned, and anyway, I didn't think it was right for a little kids' party. Instead, I pulled on a pair of overalls, stuck a straw hat on my head, and painted red circles on my cheeks with an old lipstick. I'd go as a scarecrow.

I ran downstairs and out the door, grabbed my bike, and rode as fast as I could to the hospital. On the way I thought about how much better I felt. Seventh grade wasn't all that bad, after all. I was popular there, and I could make excellent grades. Earning A's and B's was going to feel pretty good! (Not quite as good as winning first place in the art show, maybe, but good just the same.) And it didn't matter that I wasn't in the same grade as my friends. They'd be my friends, no matter what. I knew that now.

Sure enough, when I arrived at the hospital, everybody was happy to see me. The party was being held in a lounge near the children's wing, that way, even some of the youngest BSC charges could attend without breaking the hospital's rules about visitors being a certain age. The place was packed. All the BSC members were there, and all of them were in costume.

Kristy had brought Watson's portable CD player, and it was booming out dance music from the fifties. Mary Anne, dressed as Little Red Riding Hood, was dancing with Jackie Rodowsky, who wore a Frankenstein mask. He looked healthy — and happy to see so much activity in the lounge.

Stacey-the-flapper was on the dance floor, too, doing the twist near a boy in a wheelchair. And Abby, in her soccer player's outfit, seemed to be having the time of her life as she spun around carefully, holding a toddler with a broken arm.

Charlotte was there, and so were Becca

(dancing with her big sister Jessi) and the Arnold twins. I spotted Mal, playing a noisy game of slap jack with a young girl. When I took a closer look, I saw that the girl was connected by tubes to an I.V. machine, but she seemed to have forgotten she was sick, at least for the moment.

Jake Kuhn and Nicky Pike were playing Nerf baseball with a boy of about four who looked thin and pale but otherwise not too sick.

Margo and Claire were "putting on a show," entertaining three kids who were resting on a couch. The Pike girls had worn their costumes, and they were doing a Native American dance they had learned at school.

Every kid — and every baby-sitter — was smiling from ear to ear. Obviously, the Hospital Buddies Halloween party was a huge success.

I joined in the dancing, laughing out loud as I traded moves with Stacey, Kristy, Mary Anne, and Abby. At one point Mary Anne leaned toward me and whispered, "I'm so happy you came."

I was happy I'd come, too. I wouldn't have missed it for the world. I danced, I ate cupcakes, I played charades, I entered the wheelchair races; in short, I had a blast, and so did all the kids. The best part of all was when Jackie announced that he and the other kids had collected extra candy while they were trick-or-treating. At that point, each of "our" kids paired up with a Hospital Buddy and presented him with a small bag of goodies. (Naturally, we'd checked with the nurses to make sure it was all right for the kids to eat sweets.)

It was so nice to see that spirit of giving. It made me want to give something, too. So I decided something. I would donate my prize-winning painting to the children's wing at Stoneybrook General Hospital.

Finally, one of the nurses let us know that it was time to wind things up. After some tearful good-byes (and promises of future visits), we herded our charges out of the hospital.

As we stood on the sidewalk outside, Kristy proposed a special BSC meeting and pizza party that night. "I have an announcement to make," she said mysteriously. That was fine with me. I had my own announcement to make. We agreed to meet in my room at seven.

That evening, before my friends came over, I told my parents and Janine about the blue ribbon I'd received. Then I told them how much better I was feeling about being back in seventh grade — and why. My mother hugged me, my father told me he was proud of me, and Janine said she'd always known I was an artistic genius.

"But why didn't you tell us about the show?" asked my mother.

I shrugged. "I didn't think I'd win anything," I said. "I'm sorry. But the show will still be up tomorrow."

"Then we'll go see it," promised my mother. "And I hope your teacher is there. I'd like to shake her hand and thank her."

By the time my friends arrived, I'd baked a pan of brownies, popped a huge bowl of popcorn, ordered three pizzas, and set up a buffet in my room. (I was trying hard to make up for those stale pretzels I'd been serving.)

As soon as everyone was there, Kristy picked up a piece of pizza and proposed a toast. (We have a BSC tradition called the "pizza toast," when we pretend to clink our slices together. Silly, but fun.) "Here's to the BSC," she declared. "The club is back on track, and I think we proved it with our Hospital Buddies program." She paused, then lifted her slice high. "I hereby announce that our probation period is officially over!"

Whoa. What a relief. For a second, we were silent. Then we let out a cheer. "Yea!" we yelled, "clinking" our slices together.

"I have an announcement to make, too," I said, looking around the room at my friends. "First, I just want to say thank you for sticking

137

by me, even when I was having a very hard time. I know I haven't been the greatest friend lately, but that's going to change. I may be in seventh grade, but I'm still the same old Claudia."

"Yea!" everyone cried, clinking again with their slices.

"I'd also like to announce that I won — uh — first prize in my student art show," I said, trying to sound as modest as possible.

"Claud! That's excellent!" exclaimed Kristy.

"Congratulations!" said Mary Anne.

I invited everyone to come to the show the next day and see my painting. After that, we got down to the real purpose of our meeting: pigging out!

Later, as I finished off my third brownie, I looked around the room and sighed happily. The BSC was back in business, I was on top of things at school, my life was back on track. Everything felt right again.

Dear Reader,

In *Claudia Kishi, Middle School Dropout*, Claudia finds herself in a difficult situation when she is moved from eighth grade to seventh grade. Not only is she concerned about her schoolwork, but she has been moved in with a whole new group of kids. This can be difficult for anybody. I hear from lots of kids who are new in their school or town, and want to find ways to make friends. As Claudia found out, there are lots of ways to do this. One of the best is to think about things you like to do. For instance, do you like sports? Join a team at your school or in your town. Do you like art? Maybe your school is putting on a play, and you could work on the scenery or costumes. Do you feel like trying your hand at something new? See if you can take a class. Then you can meet the kids in your class. Like Claudia, you might think you're the only one in this situation. But that's not true. Everyone has been, or will be, the new kid at some point.

Happy reading,

Ann M. Martin

L. GODWIN

Ann M. Martin

About the Author

ANN MATTHEWS MARTIN was born on August 12, 1955. She grew up in Princeton, NJ, with her parents and her younger sister, Jane.

Although Ann used to be a teacher and then an editor of children's books, she's now a full-time writer. She gets the ideas for her books from many different places. Some are based on personal experiences. Others are based on childhood memories and feelings. Many are written about contemporary problems or events.

All of Ann's characters, even the members of the Baby-sitters Club, are made up. (So is Stoneybrook.) But many of her characters are based on real people. Sometimes Ann names her characters after people she knows, other times she chooses names she likes.

In addition to the Baby-sitters Club books, Ann Martin has written many other books for children. Her favorite is *Ten Kids, No Pets* because she loves big families and she loves animals. Her favorite Baby-sitters Club book is *Kristy's Big Day*. (By the way, Kristy is her favorite baby-sitter!)

Ann M. Martin now lives in New York with her cats, Gussie and Woody. Her hobbies are reading, sewing, and needlework — especially making clothes for children.

Notebook Pages

This Baby-sitters Club book belongs to _____.

I am _____ years old and in the _____ grade.

The name of my school is _____.

I got this BSC book from _____.

I started reading it on _____ and

finished reading it on _____.

The place where I read most of this book is _____.

My favorite part was when _____.

If I could change anything in the story, it might be the part when

_____.

My favorite character in the Baby-sitters Club is _____.

The BSC member I am most like is _____

because _____.

If I could write a Baby-sitters Club book it would be about ___

_____.

#101 Claudia Kishi, Middle School Dropout

Claudia is *not* happy about being moved to the seventh grade. This is what I think about Claudia's move: _____ _____ _____. If I could move any other BSC member into the seventh grade to be with Claudia, I would move _____ because _____ _____. For Claudia, one of the worst things about switching grades is that she no longer sees her friends during school. They even have separate lunch periods! When I'm at lunch, I sit with _____ _____. Eventually, Claudia makes some friends in the seventh grade. Some of my friends who are in another grade are _____ _____ _____. If I had to move to another grade, I would feel _____ _____. If I could choose one of my friends to move with me, I would choose _____. Then I'd definitely have someone to talk to during lunch!

CLAUDIA'S

Finger painting at 3...

A spooky sitting adventure

Sitting for two of my favorite charges -- Jamie and Lucy Newton.

SCRAPBOOK

...oil painting
at 13!

my family. mom and Dad, me and
Janine... and we'll never forget mimi.

Read all the books
about **Claudia**
in the Baby-sitters Club series
by Ann M. Martin

Look for #102

MARY ANNE AND THE LITTLE PRINCESS

Hannie's jaw was practically scraping the ground. "You mean, Victoria could become queen?"

"Yeah, if twenty-eight other people croak first." Linny looked at Miss Rutherford. "Right?"

Miss Rutherford gave him a tiny smile. "Yes."

Everyone started speaking at once:

"If they all catch a disease —" Druscilla began.

"She could challenge them to a duel," David Michael blurted out. "I have this cool sword —"

"If you're a princess," said Hannie, with her hands on her hips, "then where's your crown?"

"You never told us where you lived," Karen added. "A castle, or just a regular mansion?"

"Do you have, like, normal friends?" Linny added.

Andrew pointed at Miss Rutherford. "Is *she* the queen?"

Kristy was cringing. "Guys, don't you have some collecting to do? Sorry, Victoria. They're just overexcited."

"Perfectly all right," Victoria said. "And I do have friends. Lots of them. In London."

"Want to play with us?" Hannie asked.

Linny elbowed her and whispered, "Say *Your Majesty!*"

"Another time, perhaps," Victoria said.

"Yes," Miss Rutherford said briskly, taking Victoria's hand. "So nice to see you all."

As they walked away, Linny said, "Wow. She even talks like a princess."

"Why didn't she want to play with us?" Andrew asked.

Kristy wanted to scream at them. Instead she turned back to the Pilgrim village. "Come on, guys," she said with a sigh, "before we start another war with England."

100 (and more)
Reasons to Stay Friends Forever!

More titles... ▶

The Baby-sitters Club titles continued...

❑ MG48225-4	#81	Kristy and Mr. Mom	$3.50
❑ MG48226-2	#82	Jessi and the Troublemaker	$3.99
❑ MG48235-1	#83	Stacey vs. the BSC	$3.50
❑ MG48228-9	#84	Dawn and the School Spirit War	$3.50
❑ MG48236-X	#85	Claudi Kishi, Live from WSTO	$3.50
❑ MG48227-0	#86	Mary Anne and Camp BSC	$3.50
❑ MG48237-8	#87	Stacey and the Bad Girls	$3.50
❑ MG22872-2	#88	Farewell, Dawn	$3.50
❑ MG22873-0	#89	Kristy and the Dirty Diapers	$3.50
❑ MG22874-9	#90	Welcome to the BSC, Abby	$3.50
❑ MG22875-1	#91	Claudia and the First Thanksgiving	$3.50
❑ MG22876-5	#92	Mallory's Christmas Wish	$3.50
❑ MG22877-3	#93	Mary Anne and the Memory Garden	$3.99
❑ MG22878-1	#94	Stacey McGill, Super Sitter	$3.99
❑ MG22879-X	#95	Kristy + Bart = ?	$3.99
❑ MG22880-3	#96	Abby's Lucky Thirteen	$3.99
❑ MG22881-1	#97	Claudia and the World's Cutest Baby	$3.99
❑ MG22882-X	#98	Dawn and Too Many Baby-sitters	$3.99
❑ MG69205-4	#99	Stacey's Broken Heart	$3.99
❑ MG69206-2	#100	Kristy's Worst Idea	$3.99
❑ MG45575-3		Logan's Story Special Edition Readers' Request	$3.25
❑ MG47118-X		Logan Bruno, Boy Baby-sitter	
		Special Edition Readers' Request	$3.50
❑ MG47756-0		Shannon's Story Special Edition	$3.50
❑ MG47686-6		The Baby-sitters Club Guide to Baby-sitting	$3.25
❑ MG47314-X		The Baby-sitters Club Trivia and Puzzle Fun Book	$2.50
❑ MG48400-1		BSC Portrait Collection: Claudia's Book	$3.50
❑ MG22864-1		BSC Portrait Collection: Dawn's Book	$3.50
❑ MG69181-3		BSC Portrait Collection: Kristy's Book	$3.99
❑ MG22865-X		BSC Portrait Collection: Mary Anne's Book	$3.99
❑ MG48399-4		BSC Portrait Collection: Stacey's Book	$3.50
❑ MG92713-2		The Complete Guide to the Baby-sitters Club	$4.95
❑ MG47151-1		The Baby-sitters Club Chain Letter	$14.95
❑ MG48295-5		The Baby-sitters Club Secret Santa	$14.95
❑ MG45074-3		The Baby-sitters Club Notebook	$2.50
❑ MG44783-1		The Baby-sitters Club Postcard Book	$4.95

Available wherever you buy books...or use this order form.
Scholastic Inc., P.O. Box 7502, 2931 E. McCarty Street, Jefferson City, MO 65102

Please send me the books I have checked above. I am enclosing $_____
(please add $2.00 to cover shipping and handling). Send check or money order—
no cash or C.O.D.s please.

Name_____ Birthdate_____

Address _____

City_____ State/Zip _____

BSC596